I0669182

LOVE IN THE LIMELIGHT

FALLING FOR THE ACTRESS
BOOK 1

MEREDITH STONE

CONTENTS

1
_____

"You have any experience as a production assistant?"

The flustered supervisor who'd been put in charge of me weaved in and out of rows of costumes and set pieces as he lobbed questions from behind a wall of wigs.

With a large clipboard and a fully wired headset, he was intimidating to say the least.

"No," I replied, not even totally sure what the job description entailed.

"How about wardrobe—any experience there?" he called, poking his head out from between a rack of jackets.

"Not really..."

"Set design?" You could hear the frustration building in his voice.

"Nope," I muttered. I didn't even need to look in a mirror to tell that my face was the shade of the lipstick the makeup artists carried as they passed by.

"How the hell did you get this job?" he huffed. "Do you know how many people would kill to work on this movie?"

"I'm sure there would be quite a few volunteers," I sighed. I was going to be fired my first day on the job, I could feel it.

He was right—I wasn't quite sure how I landed the gig myself. 10 job interviews before graduation that led nowhere had made me desperate. When flyers for day-help started popping up on the student center jobs board, I took a shot and gave the number a call. Turns out, a former professor had written a script. One favor from my faculty friend later, and I'd somehow ended up on the set of his new movie that had taken over campus during summer break.

I knew nothing about the movies, had no idea what "day work" looked like on a set, but it was a job. And I needed a job. Desperately.

"Well, you've got to be able to fetch coffee and collect lunch orders, right?" the stressed out supervisor asked. He waited for a confirmation nod before continuing. "Okay, that is something. We don't usually do this, but I am having trouble...dealing with...her, and I really could use some help."

"Dealing with who, exactly?" I asked, not quite sure what I was getting myself into.

"Spencer Wolf—the actress. You know, the one everyone and their dog is obsessed with?"

The name sounded vaguely familiar, but for as little as I knew about movie making, I knew even less about movie stars. I'd spent an embarrassing amount of time in the library during my four years here, so I hadn't kept up with much celebrity gossip.

Not wanting to give him any more reason to fire me before I'd even started though, I nodded my head and pretended to follow along.

"She was a last minute addition to the cast, so I have been dealing with her all week. What she really needs is a personal assistant, but apparently it's difficult to find someone she likes. She's a little..standoffish. You seem like you'll be fine though. I'm going to put you on her detail the next few days. See if it works out, and if not...I don't know, hang out by the food and look like you're busy."

With that, he turned his attention back to the clipboard in his hands and seemed to forget all about me.

I played his words back through my head in an attempt to find any real job direction, but nothing stood out. The last thing I wanted was to be a bother on my first day, so I shoved my hands awkwardly in my pockets and waited for him to give me some real instruction.

I waited. And waited. And waited, until I wondered if I had turned invisible.

Finally, after minutes of standing to the side, I cleared my throat and the grumpy man looked up with a huff.

"Was there anything else you needed?" he asked. His fingers drummed the clipboard at an irritatingly rapid pace.

"Umm...you never really told me where to go," I stuttered. "Where do I find Ms. Wolf? Do I need to check in anywhere?"

"Hold on," he sighed. He flipped through a handful of pages before finding the one he wanted. "Wolf should still be in her trailer. She isn't due in makeup for a few hours. Go to the trailer lot out back; you'll find one with her name plate. Just...go in and ask if they need help."

"Okay!" I tried my best to sound chipper and happy to be working, but instead it came out overeager and shrill, neither of which were the endearing qualities I wanted to convey my first day on the job. Clipboard Man flashed me an almost pitiful look and returned to his stack of papers.

Shit, my coworkers already found me annoying.

Rather than disturb him for any more instruction, I turned around and attempted to navigate my way through the circus of production crews who had taken over the university campus that I had called home for the past four years.

I graduated just a week ago, and the movie crews wasted no time moving in for their summer shoot. I had heard rumors that the school rented out the grounds for movie sets while students were on vacation, but I had never seen it in person before.

I'd always imagined that the campus turned into a ghost-town this time of year. Maybe a few summer school students milling around, or maybe some off-season maintenance work. But this was everything but empty.

It was quite a sight to behold. It was weird seeing construction workers tearing away inside tents erected overnight. Dozens upon dozens of crew members bustled busily across every inch of campus carrying boxes filled with props and furniture pieces, and I couldn't help think how weird it was that all of this was going on just steps from dorm rooms that were usually lined with movie posters and pictures of popular actors.

I wandered around aimlessly for a few minutes, trying my hardest to sort out where the trailers might be housed, but to no avail. When I finally stumbled on a kind but intimidating looking woman with way too much makeup and the coolest hair I'd seen thus far, I bucked up the courage and asked for directions.

"Trailers are that way," she pointed with a sharpened fingernail. "Who are you looking for?"

"Spencer Wolf," I replied. "I'm supposed to be assisting her the next few days."

"Aren't you lucky. She was just named hottest up-and-coming actress under 25. You should ride that train to a full time gig if you can."

"Yeah, that could be cool," I shrugged. I had no idea if I was even going to make it a week in this gig, let alone get a full time job out of it.

"Well, good luck! Her trailer should be hard to miss. She sure is."

"Thanks," I smiled, grateful for a kind person in the midst of the chaos.

As I made my way over to the trailer lot, I pulled out my phone and did a quick search for any information I could find about Spencer Wolf.

Truth be told, I didn't know much about her apart from her growing popularity and recent role as the romantic lead in last year's biggest movie. I hadn't seen the movie, and I hadn't really thought much of the actress until I clicked over to the image section of my search.

She was gorgeous, but not in a typically Hollywood way. With her dark hair and strong features, she looked more athletic than model-esque. Tall and muscular, it was no wonder her filmography was playing roles like gymnasts or vampires or FBI agents.

To my surprise, she was only two years older than me. It was always weird meeting someone roughly your age who had achieved so much already, but I attempted to reserve my judgment and intimidation for after we met.

As I continued scrolling through information about her, I noticed a decisive trend: article after article focused on who she was dating or what she was wearing, but not a single post about her talent or acting abilities.

I scrolled through her impressive resume expecting to find any sort of accolade, but was instead greeted with what I liked to call 'hotness awards,' all those meaningless titles they give to famous people simply for looking nice in pictures.

So, she was hot and probably knew it.

That didn't usually make for the friendliest combination.

This might turn out to be a difficult few days.

2

WHEN I REACHED the sea of trailers behind the physics building, I began to scan the plaques for my actress' name. I walked past sign after sign for actors that I vaguely knew, impressed with the way my small campus had transformed into Little-Hollywood overnight.

As a poor college student the past few years, I hadn't been to the cinema in ages, so the fact that I recognized ANY of the names was a testament to the size of this production. Though I didn't know much about the film, I could see it was going to be a blockbuster.

This was no small setup.

But this was my first time being--let alone working--on a set setting. Hell, it was my first time truly working at all, let alone at a job with seemingly so many moving parts.

I was already a little overwhelmed, and I'd only been here for an hour.

I tended to spend most of my time reading or studying for classes, so I jumped at the opportunity to diversify my resume when my professor offered me the job. Having just finished my degree, I was a bit aimless and desperate for any sort of work, even if it had nothing to do with my literary degree.

When I finally got towards the end of the trailer line, I saw the handwritten sign: "Spencer Wolf."

The words were written in a haphazard manner, as if they were a second thought. The trailer was different from the others as well; it was newer and a soft tan color whereas the others were a simple white. It stood out from the others, separated her trailer from theirs, and I wondered if the actress inside would stand out just as much.

I took a deep breath and practiced my introduction over and over in my head. This was, after all, my first time meeting anyone famous, and even if I didn't know much about her, I still didn't want to seem like a bumbling fool.

Mustering all the courage in my body, I stepped up to the door and rapped my knuckles against the faux wood surface.

The dull murmur of voices quieted, and I could hear click of high heels approaching.

The door swung open, and a petite middle aged woman appeared in the opening. She was dressed casually enough with just a touch of makeup and some mysterious air of Los Angeles.

"Can I help you?" she asked, her fingers bouncing up and down on the door frame. Everyone around here seemed to be three coffees deep in energy.

"Hi," I mustered up my friendliest smile. "I am working on set and was told to come and help Ms. Wolf out with anything she might need."

The woman looked me over with a skeptical eye. "What's your name?"

"Lauren."

"Lauren...?" she pushed.

"Daly! Sorry," I stuttered. "Lauren Daly."

"Hold on just one minute." She pulled a walkie-talkie from her belt and partially closed the door.

I stepped down from the small porch to give her privacy, but I could still hear as the woman repeated my name to someone on the other end of the radio.

After an awkward few minutes waiting outside, the trailer door swung back open.

"Okay," the woman waved me inside. "You have signed all the non-disclosure forms?"

I nodded enthusiastically.

"Good. I'll probably need to have you sign a few more for if we decide to hire you. But, what the hell. We might as well give this a try; lord knows I could use some help. I'm Rebecca, by the way, Spencer's press rep."

"Nice to meet you," I smiled, shaking her hand.

"Spencer!" Rebecca called towards the back of the trailer. "Come meet your new set assistant!"

A door at the back of the trailer opened and out walked the most attractive woman I had ever seen in my life. In the smallest robe I could have imagined. My gay little eyes nearly popped out of my head.

Lordy, I hope she didn't just see me flutter.

She was tall and broad-shouldered in a way that set her apart from all the other actresses I'd seen so far, and strong in a way I had always yearned to be. She was gorgeous, but it seemed as if her femininity was more put on than natural.

I couldn't quite explain it, but there was something different in the way she moved, something about the way she held herself that was totally different from I had expected. And it somehow reminded me of the way I felt different the fall I rushed a sorority.

She felt...kinda queer.

Was it possible that the hottest actress on the scene was secretly one of us?

Or was that my little lesbian heart totally projecting?

"Hey," she smiled, her brilliantly white teeth standing out against her tanned skin. It was so strange seeing her in person just moments after I researched her online. She looked somehow even more amazing in person.

"Hi, I'm Lauren," I smiled back, trying my best to look nonchalant.

She reached forward and shook my hand, and I was immediately impressed by the strength of her grip. I'd be distracted by it, if not for all the distracting things about her.

Her incredibly distracting half-nakedness, for example.

The string that held together her robe was so loosely tied that the fabric hung low on her shoulders exposing her long neck and much of her clavicle. It was carefree and effortlessly beautiful, and it took everything in my power not to follow the lines of fabric down her body.

"This actually works out perfectly," Rebecca exhaled. Her fingers never seemed to tire from tapping against any available surface. "I have a lunch date with the studio representative in half an hour. I was going to call for a production assistant to make sure you stay on schedule, but now that we have been given Lauren to help, she can do all the escorting! Is that alright with you, Spencer?"

Spencer glanced over at me with a friendly smile, and I could see her eyes assessing whether or not I was a threat. Having her level of fame came with an inherent distrust of strangers, I was sure, and it wouldn't surprise me if she had been used before by someone new.

Trying my hardest to ease her nerves, I returned her gaze with a soft smile.

"Yeah," Spencer replied. "Lauren seems like good company for the day."

I felt the blush from before return to my cheeks at the compliment. It wasn't everyday that someone so blatantly assessed and approved of your character, especially someone so famous.

"Great! We have just killed two birds with one Lauren!" Rebecca exclaimed. In spite of all her frantic fidgeting, I had a sense that I might come to like Rebecca. "Well, I am off. Spencer, if you need me, don't hesitate to call."

The older woman leaned over and kissed the actress on the cheek before disappearing out the door in a blaze of over-caffeinated energy.

It wasn't until she was out the door that I realized she had left me without any instruction or guidance.

Not quite sure what to do next, I shoved my hand in my pocket and waited for Spencer to make the first move.

"Would you like anything to drink?" Spencer asked, moving toward the kitchenette. "We have water and soda, but I could fix you tea or coffee if you preferred that."

"I'm fine," I shrugged. "Besides, I should probably be the one fixing you tea of coffee. I'm sorry. I'm still new at this, so I may not be the best assistant just yet. I'm a really fast study though!"

"I'm actually really glad you haven't done this before. I could tell," Spencer smiled. "That's why I approved of you. I hate being treated like a child by the people I work with everyday. Or worse, my last assistant seemed to think she was my servant. No matter how much I insisted, she would NOT relax. That just makes me feel so...weird. If this works out, you better be ready to treat me like a person. I can't take anymore weirdness."

"Deal," I grinned. It was nice to speak to someone kind for a change. "I honestly have no idea what I'm doing, so this is sort of like a fresh start."

"Also," she paused, turning to look at me with suddenly very intense eyes. "Don't pre-apologize for yourself again. It's disparaging. And I'm not a fan of that. You shouldn't be either."

I was taken aback by her sudden directness. It took the air out of my lungs for a moment, and I had to take a deep breath before I nodded with a soft and surprised smile. "It won't happen again."

"Perfect," Spencer winked. "I like you already. Now, come sit with me on the couch and tell me about yourself. I don't wanna work with a stranger."

This might not be such a bad day after all.

3

I FOLLOWED Spencer to the back of the trailer which had been converted into a living room of sorts. She sat down on one side of the couch, and as I sat down across from her, she propped her feet up on the coffee table and pulled a bottle of lotion from her robe pocket.

"So, are you a student here?" she asked, squirting a glob of lotion onto her hand.

"Yeah! Or, I was. I graduated last week, but that seems like such a strange concept that I keep forgetting about it."

I watched as she rubbed the lotion on her calves and began to move her fingers in circles up her leg. The hem of the robe stretched to her mid-thigh, and as she worked her way up, so did the fabric.

I tried my hardest to be polite, but my eyes wandered down to her perfectly toned lower body. What was going on with me? I never stared at people, even if I found them attractive, but for some reason I could not keep my eyes off of Spencer.

"What did you study? Film?"

"English, actually. I'm a bit of a literature nerd," I confessed.

"I like that," Spencer looked up at me and grinned. "I've been trying to read more. Being on set is so painfully boring most days. Maybe you could make a list of books you recommend for me."

"I can totally do that! Though it might be difficult to narrow down my list of favorites," I laughed. This was going so much better than I had expected. "So, do we need to get you ready for a scene soon? Or, like, how does this work?"

"Yeah, I should probably get dressed," Spencer replied, glancing down at the clock on her phone. "When we get to set, we can ask someone for a copy of my schedule for you. Mostly, it's a lot of just keep track of schedules and making sure I stay fed. And, maybe reading some lines every once in a while."

"That sounds pretty easy to me," I sighed. Today was going a lot easier than I expected.

"Good, because ya already have the gig," Spencer laughed. "Now, where did wardrobe put my outfit for today?"

We both got up and searched the trailer closets until we found the short dress that Spencer was tagged to wear. I turned away and gave her some privacy as she discarded the robe and slipped into the dress.

Even turned away, however, I could see her silhouette out of the corner of my eye. She was fit and beautiful, and I wondered if I had already developed a girl-crush on her.

Or, a real crush...

But that would be inappropriate, and the last thing I needed on my first ever day of work.

I could honestly see the appeal of her celebrity now. I fully got it now.

"Hey, could you help me out with this stupid string? I'm terrible at tying things behind my back," she chuckled.

"Sure," I replied.

As I turned around, I tried my best to steady my hands before I reached out to assist. The top of the dress was held up by two slips of fabric meant to be tied behind the base of Spencer's neck. She was just slightly taller than me - maybe an inch or two. So my eyes hit right above her nape.

I stepped behind her and pulled her hair to one shoulder. A faint scent of lavender tickled my nose. She even smelled beautiful.

Grabbing the two strings, I tied the dress with only the slightest tremble as my fingers grazed her soft skin. Though I didn't feel nervous around her, my body had a mind of its own and a starstruck wandering gaze.

If we were going to continue to work together, I needed to release whatever this sudden pseudo-crush I had on the actress before she dismissed me like the others before.

Being this attractive was LITERALLY her job. I needed to remember that.

When we finally got her dressed and ready for her scene, I guided her through campus to the shooting location.

There was something so strange about walking in a place so familiar with someone so out of the ordinary. I pointed out the buildings where I had class to Spencer, but the campus suddenly felt more ghostlike than my real home of 4 years.

Having never been on a set before, I was surprised by the complexity of it all when we arrived at the filming location. There were people milling around, working on set details or reading through scripts, but even so, I felt lost in the crowd. Spencer was immediately whisked away by makeup artists and production assistants, and I was left to my own devices.

I didn't quite fit in, so I slumped to the back and tried to blend into the wall so I could observe in peace.

Though I didn't really have any idea what the script was about, it became clear pretty quickly that the part they were filming that afternoon was some sort of date scene. Between Spencer's skimpy dress and the absurd amount of makeup they applied to her face, I began to get the picture.

My suspicions were confirmed when I saw Chris King walk on set and make a beeline straight for Spencer.

Chris King was one of the few hot, new actors I knew simply because his face was on every advertisement and billboard released this year. It seemed as if every time I passed a magazine stand, there he was staring up at me with his baby blue eyes and perfectly manicured scruff.

I didn't blame the companies, he was extremely hot, and only more handsome in real life. I just never really understood the appeal of fantasizing over some guy so far removed from your own life.

That, and the fact that my sexuality had turned much more sapphic these last few months.

I may not be "out-out" in the world yet, but I sure as hell wasn't straight. I'd just never had the chance to date around or have any, real long-term relationship before.

Maybe I'd been too focused on succeeding at school that I'd forgotten to really live.

Or maybe I'd just had far too many unrequited crushes and stolen kisses with straight girls that I'd never allowed myself to fall for someone available.

Maybe I was just chickenshit when it came to the possibility of actually loving someone and not just reading about it.

Whatever it was, all I knew was that even a stud like Chris King did nothing for me.

As he made his way to Spencer, I watched her closely. She seemed somewhat withdrawn from the others on set, and this stiff detachment only seemed to grow worse when Chris King appeared by her side.

Even from thirty feet away, I could tell he was flirting with her. He leaned in for a big kiss on her freshly makeup-ed cheek and proceeded to swagger over her with the demeanor of a high school quarterback.

Men had a particular way of puffing themselves up when they hit on beautiful women, and in the span of five minutes, King's chest had gained three inches in protrusion.

For all the attention she was getting, Spencer sat demurely in her chair, reading over the script and replying only in pleasantries to attempts at conversation.

Even as my eyes wandered the bustling room, Spencer still stood out in every way. Amidst the handful of famous actors, she remained the most beautiful by far; yet, there was something about the way she behaved that just didn't belong. She didn't seem entirely comfortable—or perhaps she was just not interested.

When everyone had been appropriately done-up and the script properly amended, the director ushered Spencer and Chris King onto the restaurant-like set.

They sat down at a table facing across from one another, received some last minute instructions, and the filming began. I had been right, the scene was clearly a date between the two, and I watched in fascination as Spencer's whole demeanor switched as the cameras began to roll.

Spencer and Chris King ran through a few minutes of lines before the director called cut.

The second the scene ended, Spencer's forced smile faded and she exhaled deeply. Moving her head from side to side, she cracked her neck and stretched her long, muscular arms behind her back.

Chris King didn't even seem to notice Spencer's exhaustion as he picked right back up in his flirting. Reaching across the table, he grabbed her hand and spoke profusely in her direction. I could have sworn I saw her recoil.

Could Spencer be the only woman on Earth immune to Chris King?

This process repeated itself over and over until the director seemed happy and moved onto another shot of the couple. During the breaks between shots, I made my way to the craft services table at the back of the set. There were a group of technicians and assistants milling around the food, so I grabbed a bagel and stepped to the side.

I was content with carbs and observing others.

"Goddamn, she is hot," I heard one of the catering guys sigh. Without even turning around, I knew they were talking about Spencer.

"You think?" another replied.

"What, you don't think she's hot? What is wrong with you?"

"I don't know, she's just too...masculine or something."

"Are you blind?"

"No," the man defended himself. "Look, I would still totally bang her—I'm not crazy. I just prefer smaller women. She's got broader shoulders than me, and she's muscular. It just isn't very feminine, you know?"

"I guess," the first man conceded. "That doesn't mean I wouldn't do unspeakable things to her."

I thought I might gag.

I could feel my blood pressure rising just listening to the two men talk. I wanted so deeply to turn around and scold them for objectifying her, but then I would be a hypocrite for all the gawking I was guilty of in the trailer.

And honestly, I couldn't lose my job on the first day. I was having too much a good time.

Instead, I decided that I would mentally chastise the second man for disliking exactly what made Spencer so hot in my eyes: her strength. Before I could muster up the courage to actually engage with the men, however, they had disappeared.

I didn't know why their comments had bothered me so deeply, I could go online and see forum after forum of men engaged in the exact same conversation, but I felt a loyalty to Spencer after just a few hours of knowing her.

By the time I finished my bagel, the director had released the actors for a short respite. As I walked back towards the set, I saw Spencer had retreated to a back corner of the room. We made eye contact and her lips curled into a brilliant, genuine smile.

With a wave of her wrist, she motioned for me to join her in her quiet space.

"Hey," I smiled. "You did an amazing job!"

"Nah, it was silly. It's all a little silly," she shrugged. "How are you enjoying your first day, though? I know it can be horribly boring just waiting around on set."

"Not at all!" I lied. "I've really enjoyed watching the process of it all."

"Sure," she laughed knowingly. "Tomorrow we can figure out a way to help you pass the time. Maybe I can find a book you haven't already read in my small library."

"So, I passed the test? I'm hired again tomorrow?"

"Absolutely. You might be the only genuine person on this set. You aren't going anywhere if I have a say." She reached out and squeezed my hand.

I could feel a blush creep up my cheeks as I tried not to grin. I had a feeling I was going to enjoy my first job after all.

4

WHEN I ARRIVED BACK at my apartment that night, I was surprised to find my roommate, Allie, on the couch with our mutual friend and next door neighbor, Julie. The two were laughing over a bottle of wine and some popcorn, and for a moment, it felt like we were back in college. The three of us had moved into the off-campus apartment complex our Junior year and had lived in our adjoining apartments ever since.

In classic queer form, Julie and I had fooled around a little, even gone one terrible date together, our freshman year. All it took was that one awkward date to decide to remain friends, but she'd always maintained a little bit of a flirty spirit. We were closer now than we had ever been, though, and I truly counted her as one of my closest people.

A lot of our nights were spent like this: the three of us studying and sitting around talking about life.

I wondered if we would keep it up now that we all officially were graduated and moving into our next phases?

I hadn't even put down my bag before I was greeted with a barrage of questions.

"Well, how was it?" Julie asked.

"Did you meet anyone famous?" Allie added.

"Was it fun or did you wanna jump off a cliff the whole time?"

"Oh my god," I sighed, throwing myself onto the couch beside them. "It was okay. Not super exciting, but definitely a step up from a day in the library stacks. Or getting a waitress job like I was about to do."

"Oh, so it was just an okay job. How boring," Julie smirked teasingly.

"No, it was better than that!" I explained. "I actually had a really great time. The actress was nice and friendly, and I met so many cool people. It was like a mini-convention or something."

"Wait," Julie paused, throwing her hand out and onto my leg to get me to pause. "ACTRESS? What actress? I thought this was going to be, like, a you picking up craft services or cleaning up sets sorta gig!"

I laughed and leaned back into the couch, suddenly feeling more private than usual about my new job. I wasn't sure whether to brag or be cautious about sharing Spencer. I didn't want to get in trouble, but I also couldn't keep this information from my two best friends.

"Well..." I dragged out the suspense.

"Lauren!" Julie scolded. "Tell us!"

"Fine," I smiled. "I was hired to be the assistant to Spencer Wolf."

"What?!" Julie exclaimed. "I LOVE her! Allie, have you ever seen a movie with her?"

Allie shook her head, and I wasn't surprised. Allie was in her second year of med school and her free time was almost nonexistent. She was a hard worker who studied all the time. I was the only one out of the three of us who really got out and experienced campus life.

"She is so fucking hot!" Julie continued, not realizing

she'd already lost Allie. "Her legs are insane! Lauren, you have to get her to give me a personal tour of her trailer. And by tour, I mean, her bed."

"Shut up, Jules," I laughed. "You can't sleep with every hot girl you see."

"You're no fun," Julie pouted. "But seriously, are you going back to the set tomorrow?"

"Yeah," I grinned. "I actually had the best day. It was...kinda surprisingly amazing."

"Well, let's celebrate! Allie, grab another glass!"

"I can't, guys. I have to get to bed early," Allie smiled. "I have a big test tomorrow. But you should celebrate! You have your first job, Lauren, that's huge!"

Allie stood up from the couch, gave me a hug, and wished me well before disappearing into her room.

"Okay, but one glass of wine," I conceded. "Because I also need to get up early."

"Ugh, fine," Julie rolled her eyes. "You're lucky I'm tired."

We sat in comfortable silence for a moment, both sipping on our glasses of wine, and thinking.

I was thinking about the day, about the fact that I had an actual job, and the fact that I'd be back on set tomorrow morning.

And the fact that I would see Spencer again.

Julie, on the other hand, was clearly scheming.

"Lauren," Julie finally broke the silence. "Have you ever noticed anything odd about Spencer Wolf?"

"Odd?" I asked. "What do you mean, odd?"

"I don't know, there's just always something different about the way she acts in her interviews. Like, I've always noticed this little spark of...something when I watch her. Something not-so-straight."

"I had the same thought," I admitted. "I was wondering if I was totally projecting though."

"Definitely not. You should watch the interview she did for Entertainment Weekly last year," Julie grinned.

"I have, and it's not helping me at all. She's just so damn hot!"

"True, but you also can't deny the vibes."

"The vibes, huh? You're starting to sound like my mother."

"Oh, hush. You know what I'm saying."

"Yeah," I conceded. "I just never knew if that was my gayness talking or not."

"Girl, no," Julie laughed. "You might have the best lesbian-dar I have ever seen. There is no way you were just projecting."

I took a sip of my wine, and let the warmth wash over me. It had been awhile since Julie and I had sat and gossiped like this.

"Well, then, maybe she's bi?" I wondered aloud.

"I'm not sure," Julie admitted. "I've had my suspicions for years. I've never met her or anything, but I've been reading the articles about her since she started blowing up the internet. Even before she was a household name, she always seemed so guarded and secretive, you know?"

"She did seem kinda...different," I agreed.

"It's like she knows everyone is looking at her and judging her every move, so she is keeping her cards close to her chest."

"Maybe."

"But you're around her! Do you really think she could be?" Julie pressed.

"I don't know, Jules," I laughed. "I've spent, like, two hours with the girl. That isn't a lot of time to get a good read on a person."

"So, you aren't going to investigate, then?"

"No," I sighed, shaking my head. "It would be inappropriate for me to just start asking her about her sexuality."

"I bet she would be open with you about it," Julie argued. "You're the least intimidating person in the world. If she was gonna come out to anyone, it would probably be you."

"I'm not sure that's a compliment."

"It is," Julie smiled. "And you know it."

"Even if she was I would DEFINITELY NOT tell you, I'm not going to be the girl who gives away any secrets on her employer," I declared. "That's such a bad idea. It's a lawsuit waiting to happen."

"Suit yourself," Julie sighed. "Just let me know if you get any...vibes."

"I absolutely will not," I teased. "But I will say: she's way cooler than I would have expected."

"I'm really happy for ya, Lar," Julie smiled, raising her glass for a cheers. "First job, and damn - it's the coolest one we could have even dreamed up."

"Thank you, Jules. And on that note, it's time for me to go to bed so that I can keep my really cool new job for a second day."

With that, we said goodnight. Lauren retreated to her own apartment while I made my way to bed with dreams of tomorrow already on my mind.

5

I woke the next morning more excited than I'd been in a very long time.

I was dressed and out the door before Allie had even woken up, because there was no way I was going to be late for my second day on set.

I'd brought a book with me this time, knowing that there would be stretches of time where I could sit and read. Madame Bovary. A copy I'd read a dozen times, but I always loved the way it felt like longing for something more.

It was absolutely English Lit Major cliche. But what could I say? I dug it.

The set was bustling when I arrived, and Rebecca immediately spotted me from across the room. She rushed towards me, a whirlwind of energy and caffeine, and pulled me to the side.

"Spencer asked about you this morning," Rebecca whispered, grinning conspiratorially.

"She did?" I asked, not quite believing her.

"Yes! She specifically asked if you were coming back." Rebecca's finger taps had returned like a metronome against her mug. She talked fast and curt, and I suddenly felt the need to confirm whether this was good news, or if I was in trouble.

"But like...in a good way though, right?" I asked carefully.

"No, no! I mean, yes!" Rebecca assured before clarifying:,"She was asking as though she was happy you were returning."

"Oh," I smiled, blushing slightly. "That's sweet."

"It is!" Rebecca agreed. "But don't get too excited. She is still very private and guarded, so you may never be able to read her completely. But she is loyal as hell if she likes you."

"I know," I shrugged. "I wasn't expecting that. But, it's still nice to feel wanted."

"Well, don't expect that from everyone," Rebecca warned. "A lot of people in this business are not nearly as warm as Spencer is. She's a special case, and I am sure they won't all be as welcoming. I've seen many a good assistant run from a set crying when they realize the truth of this industry."

"That makes sense, though," I replied. "Spencer is young and trying to make a good impression. These older people have been around the block and have learned to protect themselves. Their shields are up for a reason."

"True, but don't get all sappy on me, kid," Rebecca winked. "You have a tough hide, and Spencer has taken a liking to you. This is a good thing. I just didn't want you to get too caught up in your own feelings and take something wrong. It can be confusing and overwhelming, so just keep an open mind."

"Thanks," I replied. "I will."

"Good. Now, let's go find her."

I followed Rebecca through the crowd actors and assistants until we arrived at the makeup and wardrobe department. I was surprised to see Spencer already sitting in a chair having her makeup touched up, but the second she spotted me, her entire face lit up.

"There she is!" Spencer exclaimed, pointing a finger in my direction. "My personal assistant, back for a second day!"

"Here I am," I laughed, suddenly embarrassed. "Did you think I wouldn't come back?"

"I wasn't quite sure. A lot of people don't," she smiled. "But I was hoping you would."

"Oh, she's just been with me," Rebecca interjected. "I had a few things to discuss with her. I hope that's okay."

"Of course, of course," Spencer replied. "Thank you for returning her to me."

"You got it, boss," Rebecca shot finger guns Spencer's way, and I think it was the first time I'd ever heard either of them laugh. They were clearly close.

"I'll get you some coffee," Rebecca turned to me. "Coffee, Lauren?"

"That would be great, thanks."

"So, I have good news and bad news," Spencer said as soon as Rebecca was out of earshot.

"Oh god," I sighed.

"The bad news is that the schedule has changed," she explained. "My scenes got moved from later in the day to right now. So, we are going to be filming the last scene we did yesterday, but in reverse order."

"Oh, okay," I nodded, not entirely sure how this was a bad thing.

"And the good news is that now, we have more time to kill while the crew sets everything up," Spencer smiled. "So, I brought you a book from very tiny, but well loved book collection. I left it in my trailer in hopes that you'd be back today."

She said the words so excitedly yet somehow casually all

at once, and I had to take a moment to process what she had just said.

"You brought me a book?" I asked, quite frankly more shocked than anything.

"Of course, silly!" she smiled. "Promised I would. Only problem is - it's in my trailer still. We'll have to grab it later, sorry."

"That's actually amazingly hilarious because: I brought a book myself," I laughed. "So we will have options."

"No. Fucking. Way," she said with a grin that brought a moment of something almost surprised to her eye. "I guess great minds really do think alike. So tell me, what did you bring to read?"

I held up the cover of my book, and her smile widened.

"I've always wanted to read that," Spencer mused.

"It's one of my favorites," I grinned. "What did you bring?"

Spencer shook her head with a mischievous grin. "I think that should be a fun surprise for after we finish that one. Make sure you keep coming back around. Do you think you could read a bit to me while they fix me up?"

The question took me slightly aback. She was doing that a lot this morning.

I'd never actually been asked to read to anyone before, I realized. It felt very personal for some reason. And yet, the question didn't sound odd at all coming from her.

"If you'd like."

"Please."

So, as they went to work on her hair and makeup, I began to read the story out loud, watching her expression closely. It was interesting to watch her become absorbed by the story, and even more so when she asked questions about the characters or the plot.

When they were done with her makeup, and ready to

dress her, she asked me to keep reading, so I kept going. I sat in the corner and continued reading aloud, and Spencer remained silent, listening attentively as they dressed her.

When she was fully decked out, the wardrobe stylist excused herself to grab a prop and I finished the chapter.

"Wow," Spencer mused. "That is such beautiful writing. I love the imagery of it all."

"That's my favorite part, I think," I replied. "I heard, once, that Flaubert used to yell his sentences out loud to make sure they sounded beautiful. No idea if that's true, or just some English Major fable, though."

"Who cares if it's true or not. That is fucking badass!"

Spencer glanced at me once last time as she walked towards the trailer door. Her eyes sparkled, and I couldn't quite tell if it was the makeup or some spark in them, but they were beautiful.

She was beautiful.

She shot me a smile and a beacon of her hand. "Alright, come on. We've gotta get to set. But, you better know that this is our new filming tradition."

I let her lead the way out so she wouldn't see the smile that was now probably stupidly splashed across my face.

I'd never wanted to read more.

6

THE NEXT WEEK flew by in a blur. Everyday was a new adventure as I learned more and more about the film process and more and more about Spencer.

Most of my time was spent hanging around set or helping Spencer practice her lines, and the few times I was sent to run errands, I actually missed being around for the action more than I enjoyed having an actual task.

Even when it was boring, there was something so mesmerizing about watching Spencer work.

By Friday, I was exhausted, but having the best time with her.

We were sitting around her trailer, reading and talking about nothing and doing our best to pass the time until the end of the day. Earlier in the week, we'd started an intense, marathon game of tic-tac-toe to keep us busy, but neither that nor Madame Bovary were keeping us properly entertained on this particular Friday afternoon.

"So, what is there to do around here on a weekend night?" Spencer asked.

She placed her elbows on her knees and leaned forward.

I could see the excited little girl in her when she sat like that. And she only seemed to do it in the confines of the trailer.

"Not much," I admitted. "It's mostly a college town, so the bars are almost totally aimed at that underage drinking demographic. Besides, they'll be pretty dead with all the students gone."

"Barf. Chris will love that, though. He feeds off the attention of 18 year old girls with a need to be accepted. He's so gross; he has probably fucked half the crew by now." She paused and thought for a moment. "He hasn't come onto you, has he?"

"No," I laughed. "I don't think he would look my way even if I wanted that."

"Would you want that?" she pried. There was something timid in her question that I'd not heard from her before.

"No, he is definitely not my type," I replied quickly. I desperately wanted her to know that I was in no way attracted to Chris, but I wasn't quite sure whether we were at the level of professional vs friendship where I could tell her just how gay I had realized I was.

She seemed to mull the words over in her head. Her eyes were staring at me so intently that I suddenly felt self-conscious of my poorly applied makeup and dark eye-bags. There wasn't judgement in them, though.

Was it curiosity? Puzzling me out?

I wanted to know what she was thinking, but I didn't have the courage to ask.

"Well, I'm starving," she sighed, changing the subject and rubbing her stomach in an adorably dramatic fashion. "Would you want to get some dinner?"

"As in, together?" I stuttered. We'd had food in groups on set before, but never what I'd consider "together."

"No, at LEAST two tables apart," she laughed. "Of course together, silly! It's not that shocking, is it?"

I chuckled, shaking my head. "No, I just never would have thought you'd want to..."

"Want to, what?" she pressed.

"I don't know - hang out with someone like me?" I felt myself stumbling over my words. "Most of the talent acts like their above me here. You're so much different from them in that way."

Spencer sat back with a soft laugh, "Wow! I think that might be one of my best reviews to date! Usually I'm called a bitch or cold. Especially with others on set."

"Well, all the other assistants spend half the day trashing their talent, so I think you're pretty damn great by comparison," I teased.

"Well, thank you. But, for the record, I don't think of you as 'my assistant.' That seems so dismissive." She looked at me deeply and sincerely. Once again, she reached out and squeezed my hand, but this time her fingers lingered just a few seconds longer than I expected. "Now, where should we go to eat?"

I suggested a few of my favorite local haunts, and we quickly agreed on a small diner close to my apartment. Spencer offered to call her studio provided private car, but I suggested we just take mine from set.

It took Spencer 5 minutes to get ready. She put her hair back in a bun and threw on a baseball cap. Rather than the dress she had rocked all afternoon, she slipped into a pair of comfy, loose jeans and an oversized sweatshirt with the university logo across the front. I wondered when she'd picked that up, and I suddenly had the hilarious image of Rebecca in the campus store running through my mind.

If I didn't know who she was, I would have assumed she was just another college girl fresh off a studying binge.

How did she still look stunning in jeans, though?

"Alright, I'm ready!" she exclaimed.

I could tell from the glint in her eye that she was excited to be out of her little bubble for a while.

It wasn't until we got to my car, however, that I realized how embarrassingly old it was. I was about to be driving an international movie star around in a ten year old beater with books and spare notepads still strewn around the backseat.

"Uhh, maybe we should call the car after all," I suggested, backpedaling quickly.

"No. Not a chance," she giggled. "Do you know how long it's been since I've been able to drive around with friends and blast stupid music? I can't fucking wait!"

"Okay, but you've been warned about my car."

As we got in, she marveled at everything, as if she was in a museum. She reached for the old-school radio dial until she'd found the perfect channel, and suddenly music was blasting through my shitty speakers. As a Queen came on, she sang out in a voice that was painfully off-pitch, but there wasn't the slightest hint of embarrassment in her actions.

I couldn't help but giggle; it was so normal that it was almost shocking.

Who was this woman?

She flipped through the radio stations until she found one that played hits from the '90's. A popular girl group came on, and she squealed with delight. As she began to belt the words, I just sat back laughing and observing.

"Oh, come on!" she yelled, reaching out and shaking my arm. "You know the lyrics. You have to sing with me!"

I was never one for singing in public, even in my own car, but around her I felt different. I took a deep breath and let loose. She was right; I did know every single word. We sang together in a strangely harmonized atrocious tone.

As we sang, I couldn't help but look over and smile at my rambunctious passenger in the front seat. She was like a child on the playground dancing around after having been cooped up all day.

The drive to the diner shouldn't have taken more than ten minutes, but I took a few detours just to prolong the trip.

I didn't want this moment to end.

By the time we finally got to the diner, Spencer was worn out from her show. "Whoo," she sighed. "I need some pancakes."

"Me too," I laughed.

We made our way inside and were seated at an old-school booth by an elderly woman with a coffee-stained smile. After giving us a few minutes of looking over the menu, she returned with coffee and a hand on her hips.

"Good afternoon, darlings. What can I get for you?"

"Could I get a stack of chocolate chip pancakes?" Spencer asked. "Oh, and a milkshake!"

"Sure thing! What about you, hunny?"

"I'll have the same," I smiled.

"Coming right up!"

As soon as the woman left, Spencer turned her attention to me with a sparkle in her eyes and a giant grin. "I don't think you understand how excited I am. I've been dieting the last month for the action scene we shot yesterday, and I am starving for carbs."

"Well, this place makes the best pancakes I have ever eaten. You are in for a treat."

"Wonderful!"

I hadn't seen Spencer smile so much in the entire week I had worked with her.

"How do you manage to diet like that?" I asked.

"Ugh," she groaned. "It is the worst. I appreciate my job —don't get me wrong—but the whole dieting aspect drives me crazy. Like, I'm playing an action star who starves to death. That's the kind of shit I hate about the industry."

Spencer looked at me softly and continued, "You must think we are so silly. I mean, all I do everyday is run around in costumes pretending to be someone else. I can't imagine what someone like you must think."

"What does that mean? Someone like me?" I cocked my eyebrow.

"I don't know, someone intelligent, someone good hearted. It all must seem frivolous to you."

"Do you not think films can matter?" I asked, slightly taken aback by this sudden shift in her tone.

Spencer sat back in the booth, quietly mulling over my question. I'd started to notice the soft wrinkle that would fury her brow when she was lost in thought like this. It was undeniably adorable, and a face she hid most of the time.

"No, I do," she finally replied. "I just think the things I have been forced to work on are all silly. I'm so sick of playing shallow female characters. I want to play someone important or a character with actual depth."

"Why can't you?" I asked. "I'm sure you could land any role you wanted."

"It's much easier said than done. When I first started, I was so much pickier. I would only pick a project if it met my 'specific code.' Then I realized I was working for a lot of people, you know? It isn't just me at the end of the day. I am working for my agents, my assistants, hell, even my own family. They depend on me to make money, and money just isn't available in the arthouse side of film."

"Yeah," I replied softly. "I guess I had never really thought about that side of the business."

"I'm not saying everyone is bad. I mean, you've met the people on set. Everyone is just trying to work hard and do their best for their families. I just wish at the end of the day that I could make a difference. I want to play the roles that inspired me as a kid. When I think back, it wasn't the Hollywood ideal of a woman as a prop for a man that made me want to be an actress. It was the strong female characters with actual substance that inspired me. I guess I just want to inspire people."

"Maybe you have," I shrugged. "Hell, you have changed my opinion of the industry."

"Really?" she asked eagerly. Her eyebrow cocked in an adorable question.

"Yeah, I never thought this would be as important as it feels. I honestly did see it as silly before I came to work on set. You are much different than I thought you would be."

"Oh yeah?" she smiled. "So you do like me? I was starting to wonder after the first couple of days."

"Of course I do!" I exclaimed. "I have been told that I'm a little hard to read, but I promise I like you."

"You are," she agreed, "but I appreciate it. I have people kissing my ass all day, so it was surprising to meet someone like you. You aren't fake, and that is something rare in this industry. You are a breath of fresh air."

Before we had the chance to say anything else, our food arrived. Two large stacks of chocolate chip pancakes and two even bigger milkshakes took up the majority of the table. I wondered if Spencer and her LA sensibilities had realized what she was getting into. We took our pancakes seriously here.

To my surprise, though, she dove into them without regret or hesitation. Before I was through two, she had finished the entire plate and scarfed down her milkshake to boot.

"Wow, you really were hungry," I giggled.

"You know what they say: beauty is pain. I suffered quite a bit without carbs this month."

We talked about everything as we finished our meal. From my previous classes to my group of friends, she wanted to know everything there was to know about me. I had never experienced such considerate inquisition before, but it was nice. She cared about what I had to say, and that was a unique feeling.

After we had exhausted both the conversation and our friendly waitress, she brought us the bill and Spencer reached to pay without hesitation. I protested out of habit, but she wouldn't even listen. I watched as she reached into her clutch and rifled through her wallet. She had the bill in her lap, and I could tell that for some reason she didn't want me to see what she was doing.

This, however, only made me more curious. I tried my best to hide my gaze, and I was surprised to see her pull out what looked like a few hundred-dollar bills and stuff them quickly into the plastic envelope. I didn't know it was possible, but I suddenly liked her even more. A few hundred dollars meant nothing to someone like Spencer, but it would make our waitress' week.

Before the waitress returned to the table, Spencer dragged me out of my seat and back to the car.

"So, where should I take you?" I asked.

"I guess back to my hotel room. That is, unless you want to invite me back to your apartment," she teased.

I considered it for a moment, but then I realized my two roommates would likely ruin any situation that I imagined. They were terrible hosts even under the best of circumstances. Plus, they had already bugged me about Spencer enough. The last thing I needed was for them to embarrass me in front of her.

"How about a raincheck on the apartment visit?" I asked. "I should probably just drop you off at the hotel."

Spencer climbed into the car, but there was a look of disappointment on her face. I wondered if she wanted me to invite her after all.

It only took a few minutes to get to her hotel. There weren't very many options in town, and the studio had put her up in the nicest.

"Do you want to come in?" she asked, stepping out of the car.

"I should probably get home. I'm pretty exhausted after all those carbs," I sighed. I had no idea why I said it. The words had slipped out of my mouth and I instantly regretted them.

"Oh. Right."

The same look of sadness flashed in her eyes, and I wondered why the fuck I had not just said yes. It wasn't that I didn't want to hang out, I was just suddenly aware of how nervous Spencer made me in the best way.

"Well, anytime you want to hang out here, you are more than welcome. Maybe we could have a sleepover soon," she winked, bouncing back from her momentary quietness.

I felt something churn in my stomach that I couldn't quite explain. It was the same feeling I had gotten when my friend Stacy had braided my hair in middle school. My whole body tingled.

There was something about Spencer, something about the way she talked to me and looked at me that made my knees weak. At first I had passed it off as a girl-crush, but now I was beginning to wonder if there wasn't something more. I had always considered myself queer, but I'd never really acted on it. I'd never really acted on anything.

I'd been working hard to keep my gut flutters professional around Spencer, but perhaps there was something more simmering under the surface.

Before I could change my mind or her withdraw her offer, I decided to take a leap of faith.

"Wait, what is I saying? It's a Friday night. I may not be

able to have a sleepover, but I would absolutely love to come up for a drink," I announced.

Smiling, I could see the excitement from earlier in the evening return to Spencer's eyes. "Well, what are we waiting for? I have a whole full bar ready to be torn into in my suite upstairs!"

7

WE VALETED the car as Spencer led me into the lobby of our town's only "posh" hotel. It certainly wasn't The Ritz, but it was surprisingly beautiful. With a grand lobby that led into a speak-easy style private entrance to the upper floor suites, it was the clear choice when the studio was looking for floors to rent for the film's stars.

Somehow, Spencer seemed to know all of the night-crew staff on a first name basis. The bellhop and doorman greeted her enthusiastically. The desk clerk, who couldn't have been older than I, nearly fainted when he saw her.

"Hi, Joe!" Spencer greeted him, as she took in his star-struck gaze.

"Hi, Miss Wolf!" He grinned from ear to ear, his voice cracking as he spoke. "Welcome back! Can I call for the concierge for you? Anything for your or your guest?"

"No, thanks thought! We are just going to have a few drinks to round out a lovely pancake dinner," Spencer explained. "But, we will call down for something to eat later if we somehow get hungry again tonight."

"I'm sure that can be arranged," he beamed. "Enjoy your night!"

"Thank you, Joe!" Spencer called out as we walked into the elevator. Turning to me, she grinned, "The team here is great. Some times I'l come down and hang out the lobby bar if I get bored at night."

I watched the exchange as one of those grins that just can't help itself tugged at my lips. "You're just, like, so awesome."

She smiled warmheartedly then turned quickly back to the door as the elevator binged open onto her floor. I wasn't sure, but I thought I could see a tint of pink on her neck. I'd never seen Spencer blush though. I kinda wanted to see it again.

"This is me," she nodded towards the large double doors at the end of the hall. They were twice the size of the others in the hall and looked like the grand entrance to the sort of sanctuary fitting of Spencer. Bold. Beautiful. Slightly mysterious.

She walked ahead of me to her door, pulling her keycard from her clutch as we got there. As she did, her sweater rode up her back slightly, exposing a tiny sliver of her pale, creamy skin. I felt the heat rise up in my cheeks, and I had to turn away and distract myself.

"This place is amazing," I said, looking around. "They put you in the penthouse suite? Wow."

"It's not so bad," she shrugged.

The entryway of the suite was the size of my entire apartment. To the right, a set of sliding double doors led out onto a private terrace, complete with a hot tub and breathtaking view of the mountains.

"Wow," I repeated, not being able to find any other word.

"Make yourself comfortable," she offered. "I'm going to freshen up a bit, but I'll be right back."

I watched as she headed off down the hallway. She walked with a confident grace, her hips swaying seductively.

My mind wandered as I stared at her from behind. What was it about this woman that made me feel so weak?

I looked around the room for the first time, taking it all in. Everything was perfectly put together. The kitchen was sleek and modern with marble countertops and top of the line appliances. In the center, there was a bar set up with two stools.

"Do you want a drink?" she called out. "I'm pretty good at making cocktails."

"That sounds perfect," I replied, settling onto one of the leather sofas in the living room. "Can I help you at all?"

"Nope," she exclaimed. "I have this bartending thing down."

I sat back, relaxing for the first time all week. The sofa was soft and comfy, and it was a nice change of pace to be off my feet. The view out the window was magnificent, and the moon was full and bright. It lit up the room with a beautiful blue light.

A few moments later, Spencer walked over and handed me a gin and tonic with a flourish. She had a matching drink in her other hand.

"Here you go. This is one of my favorites. If you like, there are some fun things in the mini-bar, too. Make yourself comfortable.

"You really know how to mix a drink," I laughed, taking a sip of the cool beverage. "Wow, this is good. So, did you get a lot done today?"

"Yes," she sighed, "but I'm sick of running the same scene over and over. It's getting really boring. What did you think?"

"I loved it," I replied.

"Liar," she giggled.

"No, really, it was good. The tension between you and Chris was palpable. I was really into the storyline."

Spencer snorted a huffy laugh. "It's not hard to capture tension between Chris and I. The trick is making it look flirty rather than frustrated."

"You really aren't a fan of his, are you?" I asked, surprised at how open she was now that we were behind closed doors.

She smiled knowingly again. "Let's just say, he's not really my cup of tea. The studios and agents and basically everybody has been trying to force us together as some PR stunt for years though. Management has been looking for the right movie for years for us to star in together. When Becca-what's-her-name dropped out, the teams jumped on the opportunity to finally get us on screen together."

"It's wild how much goes into the backend of productions," I murmured, taking a sip of my half-finished drink. "So much stuff I never even considered. How many people must see these movies every day without ever realizing what goes into the backend."

"Yeah," Spencer sighed. "And how many people see scenes between Chris and I - or even worse, the pictures we'll have to take during the press tour, and assume we're a thing."

"You all do have amazing acting chemistry," I replied. "So, I get the confusion."

"That's just the job, ya know?" Spencer shrugged. "And, it's not like I hate him. He's not a bad guy. He's just a bit of a vapid fuckboy, and that is DEFINITELY not my type."

She let out a soft laugh as she finished her drink. "Want another?"

"Sure," I replied, taking one last swig from my own glass. "So, it's just good acting, huh? The tension with Chris on camera?"

"Well, I'm glad you think it's 'good' acting," Spencer laughed. "But yeah, it's all a show. All of it is. The paparazzi pics, the public relationships, the even more public breakups. All organized PR."

"I guess that's the price of fame, huh?"

"Yeah," she shrugged. "It's part of the business. It's all part of the business. Even the fucking. Hell, the fucking is a huge part of it. But it's never real, not when it's part of a movie or a film or a publicity stunt."

"Never?" I asked, curious.

"Almost never," she smirked, looking me up and down. "There is the occasional person that is a bit different, but not often. I have the pleasure of being stuck on this movie set with two of those people. Well, one is an absolute douche. But the other, she's pretty incredible."

"Is she?" I asked, unable to stop the corners of my lips from turning upward.

"Yeah, I've met a couple of people like her throughout the years," she replied, a slight blush rising in her cheeks. "One or two. People that make me forget it's just a business. People that make me think about what it would be like to date a woman.

"But it's just so rare to meet someone you truly connect with."

"It is," I sighed, thinking of my last ex. He was sweet, but it was never that kind of connection.

"Sometimes you have to take a leap," she suggested. "Or, maybe you just need to get laid."

"Excuse me?"

"What?" she grinned mischievously. "Don't tell me you haven't noticed me looking."

My breath caught in my throat, and suddenly my stomach felt like a thousand butterflies had just been set loose.

"I mean, yeah," I stumbled. "But I thought you were just, umm... Well, I didn't know if you were being nice or..."

"Or?" she pressed.

"Maybe testing me?"

Spencer's mouth curved into a soft smile. She looked down at her drink as she swirled it around, staring deeply into its amber liquid.

"No, Lauren," she began. "I've definitely not been 'testing' you. I don't really have to, I can usually tell when someone is attracted to me."

"Oh," was all I managed to utter. I had no idea what to say.

"Well," Spencer shrugged, "this is awkward. I've misread this entire situation. Maybe you don't like women after all."

"I do," I said quickly.

"Are you sure? I've gotten mixed signals. You're not even sure."

"No, no," I rushed. "I'm sorry, you just surprised me, that's all. I guess I wasn't expecting the conversation to go there. I'm usually very private about this sort of thing, and I'm not exactly experienced with, you know, other women."

"Really?" she asked. "But, you're so beautiful."

I felt myself flush as the compliment hit me like a ton of bricks. No one had ever called me beautiful. It was shocking and exciting and scary.

"So are you," I finally whispered.

"Thanks," she smiled, the sparkle in her eye returning.

"But, well, you know, I'm not gay," I tried to explain. "I mean, I've been attracted to girls before, but I've only really been with men. I mean, I had a crush on a girl in college, but I never did anything about it."

"You can be bisexual," she offered.

"I know," I admitted. "I'm not even sure that I am. I mean, I've always considered myself queer. But, well, it's a small town, and there's not really a lot of options for someone like me."

"Hmmm, well, I would say that your experience is lacking. And, I can tell by your body language and tone that you are a little bit turned on right now."

"What?!" I blurted. "How can you tell that?

"Body language," she explained. "It's not that hard, actually. Your chest is flushed, your pupils are dilated, and you've started biting your lip. Those are the biggest signs."

"Well, that's embarrassing."

"Don't be," she smiled. "It's a nice look on you."

"It's not fair," I replied, taking another sip of my drink.

"What isn't?"

"I have no idea what your tells are," I answered.

"Well," she began, "you can ask me. If you'd like, that is."

"Really?"

"Yes," she nodded, her voice suddenly low and husky.

"Well, okay," I said.

"Good," she grinned.

"So, what are they then?"

"My tells?"

"Uh huh."

"I guess you'll just have to figure them out," she replied, a wicked grin tugging at the corners of her mouth.

"That's not fair," I laughed.

"Life's not fair, sweetheart. It's not my fault you don't have the advantage."

"You know," I continued, "we have been drinking for hours now, and you still haven't told me anything about yourself."

"That is a total lie!" she said, feigning offense. "I have told you plenty. Besides, what do you want to know?"

"Okay, fine. Tell me something else, then. Something I don't already know."

She thought for a moment and then replied, "I used to sing."

"You did?"

"Yep, from the time I was six. My mom put me in singing lessons. She's the one who encouraged me to do the auditions and pageants and stuff."

"Really? That's so young! Did you want to do that, or did she make you?"

"Oh, no," she assured me. "I loved it. It was something I did with my mom. Plus, she would give me spending money for each pageant and audition."

"So, you did it for the spending money?"

"Nah, it was just the best way to spend time with her, ya know? My dad's an asshole, so he was always out doing stuff. We never saw him unless he wanted us to watch him play golf or some shit. And, well, my older brother was always out being a dickhead with his friends. So, it was a good excuse to hang out with her."

"Your brother sounds like a blast," I giggled. "What's his name?"

"Michael," she sighed. "He's an absolute shit."

"Older brothers can be like that. I'm sure he cares about you."

"I'm not," she snorted. "But, yeah. So, what about you? What's your family like?"

"Oh, I'm an only child," I explained. "My parents are both teachers. I'm pretty close with them. We aren't a huge, happy family or anything, but we get along. They are both really supportive.

"I bet they are! What do they do? Your parents, I mean."

"My mom teaches English," I shrugged. "She was actually a journalist when she was younger, but she gave that up when she got pregnant with me. My dad teaches science. He's a geologist. He's also a professor at the local university."

"Oh wow," Spencer replied. "Do they know you are, you know, gay?"

"Sort of. They have suspicions, I'm sure. But, I've never really dated anyone for long enough to bring them around. It's a small town. They'd have their own assumptions and prejudices, I'm sure. And, my dad's not the most open-minded person. So, yeah, not a conversation I'm looking forward to having. What about your parents?"

"Not really. They live in Seattle. We aren't close. But, they're not homophobic either. At least, not as far as I can tell."

"That's good."

"Yeah, they are pretty liberal," she replied, a hint of sadness creeping into her tone.

We sat in silence for a few minutes, sipping our drinks. I could feel the warmth spreading through my body. The alcohol was making me relaxed, and I leaned back against the sofa, letting out a long sigh.

"It's late," I finally said.

"Is it?" she asked, glancing at the clock on the wall. "Shit, you're right. I have an early call time tomorrow. You can crash here if you want. There's plenty of room."

"Oh, no," I began. "I can't let you do that. I don't want to intrude."

"You won't be," she assured me. "Seriously. It's not a big deal."

I looked around the suite, unsure of how to respond. Part of me wanted to stay, but another part was scared about what would happen if I did.

"Maybe next time," I smiled. "I've got an early morning running errands with my roommate. She'll freak if I'm not there when she wakes up. She watches way too much Law and Order."

"Next time," she laughed.

"Well, it is a long drive home."

"Yes, it is. Will you text me when you get there? Or, at least, wake up to text me?"

"Yeah," I agreed. "I'll text you in the morning."

"Good."

"Okay," I said, rising to leave.

Spencer followed me to the door. We stood there for a moment, looking at each other. I felt an intense mix of emotions welling up inside me. Excitement, confusion, and fear all surged through me.

I didn't know what to say or how to say it.

"Thank you for dinner," I finally said.

"You're welcome. Thank you for coming."

Without another word, Spencer leaned forward and gave me a soft kiss on the cheek, close to the corner of my lips. Her fingers lingered on my shoulder even as she pulled away.

"Goodnight, Lauren," she purred, stepping back and leaning against the door frame.

"Night, Spencer."

With that, I turned and made my way to the elevator before I melted into a puddle right on the hotel floor.

8

I MADE my way through the hotel lobby and towards the valet, where I found my car already waiting for me. They really were full service here.

Sliding into the driver's seat, I started the car and began driving home on auto-pilot. My mind was still spinning from the wild night with Spencer. From pancakes to singing in my car to seeing her in her private sanctuary, I couldn't believe this was how the evening had turned out - especially after such a boring morning.

The moon was bright as it illuminated the road ahead, and I drove in silence, trying to process everything that had just happened. There was no question that Spencer was attractive. But, now, there was no doubt she was attracted to me, too.

When she had first invited me up to her room, I hadn't been sure what she meant. Now, I was certain. And, it made me wonder why I had left.

I knew the reasons were probably right, but that didn't make it any easier. As the hotel and Spencer got farther and farther away, I couldn't help but feel a sense of longing.

There was a connection between us, something undeniable and electric. And, I was pretty sure Spencer felt it, too.

As I drove through the dark streets, I replayed the night's events in my mind. The way she looked at me, the way she spoke to me. It was like no one had ever looked at me before. And, I had to admit, it was a little overwhelming.

"Ugh, get it together," I groaned aloud, rolling my eyes.

I had no idea what I was doing. This was all so new to me. And, I wasn't sure if I was ready for it.

I thought about the way her lips had brushed my cheek as she kissed me goodbye. It had been so gentle and tender. No one had ever kissed me like that before.

"Get a grip, Lauren," I mumbled, shaking my head.

I knew it was stupid to get caught up in the moment. After all, we had only just met a few days ago. Still, I couldn't help but think about the way she had made me feel.

"She's just a woman," I said aloud, trying to reassure myself.

But, Spencer wasn't just a woman. She was a celebrity. And, she was a lesbian.

Lesbian.

The word echoed in my head as I pulled into my apartment parking lot.

I had never seriously dated a woman before. Sure, I'd had crushes and flings here and there, but real romance? Real, serious, feelings? This overwhelming desire? This part was foreign to me still.

As I walked up the stairs to my apartment, I couldn't stop thinking about Spencer. Her eyes, her smile, her laugh. The way she looked at me, like I was the only person in the world.

And, her lips. Those perfect, soft, pink lips. I could imagine what they would feel like against mine.

The thought made my heart race. I took a deep breath and opened the front door, trying to compose myself.

"Hey, girl! Where have you been all night?" Julie exclaimed.

"Out," I replied, trying to keep my voice steady.

"Clearly," Julie laughed. "So, did you go out with the hot actress or what?"

"Ummm... yeah, kinda," I admitted.

"Oh, my god, Lauren! That is awesome!"

"I don't know," I sighed, feeling the butterflies in my stomach return.

"What's wrong? Don't tell me you blew it?"

"No," I laughed, "I didn't blow it. In fact, I think it went really well. Better than I could have ever imagined. She's so... I don't know. She's amazing, Jules. She's so funny and interesting. And, she's smart, too."

"So, what's the problem then?"

"The problem is," I continued, "that I have no idea what the hell I'm doing. This is all so new to me. It's just a bit overwhelming, you know?"

"Ahhhh," Julie nodded. "I see."

"What should I do, Jules? What do you think I should do?"

"I think," she began, "that you should do what makes you happy. That's what matters most, right?"

"I guess," I shrugged.

"Look, Lauren," Julie said, taking a deep breath. "You're a grown woman. You're allowed to explore your own desires, whatever they may be. If you're attracted to this woman, then you should go for it. You've spent way too long focused on the future and forgetting to live in the present."

"Really?" I asked.

"Yes," she affirmed. "Absolutely."

I sat there, absorbing her words.

"Well, thank you, Julie," I finally said. "You are a great friend."

"I try," she laughed. "Now, go get some sleep. I'm sure you have a big day ahead of you tomorrow."

"I do," I sighed. "Thanks, again. Goodnight."

"Goodnight, Lauren."

I walked down the hall and collapsed into my bed, the events of the evening finally catching up with me. It had been an exhausting and exhilarating day, and I couldn't believe how much had changed.

I had gone from a normal, everyday college graduate to a personal assistant for a Hollywood star. I had seen behind the scenes of a major movie production and made friends with a beautiful, famous actress.

I could hardly believe it was all real. It felt like a dream. A wild, unbelievable, amazing dream.

I drifted off to sleep, my thoughts filled with Spencer and the possibilities of the future.

Julie was right. I had spent too long ignoring any fun or impulsivity. It was time to actually start enjoying life, and I couldn't deny that I enjoyed Spencer more than I ever could have imagined.

9

THE NEXT WEEK AT WORK, Spencer was even friendlier than usual. As we hung out in her trailer, she would reach out and grab my hand or touch me whenever she could. I wasn't complaining, it was the nicest contact I had in a long time.

It was like some barrier had been broken by pancakes, and suddenly we weren't Ms. Wolf, the famous actress, and Lauren, her assistant, anymore. We were just us—at least in the confines of the trailer.

Even though I knew nothing would happen—she was a fucking movie star after all—my mind would wander every single time she laughed just a little extra hard at my jokes or leaned on me when we ran her lines.

What the hell was happening to me? I was developing a serious crush on someone five times out of my league.

I got so caught up in our friendship the following Friday afternoon that I forgot to check the set schedule. On any other day, I would have known the times of her shoots by heart, but for some reason that day I couldn't take my eyes off of her. My mind was a single track train and she was my sole focus.

We were in the middle of a conversation when, with a

sinking feeling in my gut, I looked up at the clock. It was well past noon. Scrambling through my binder, I realized with horror that Spencer had been due on set nearly an hour ago.

"Fuck!" I yelled.

"What's wrong?" she asked. Concern flashed in her eyes as she reached her hand out towards me.

"You are overdue on set."

"Oh, shit," she sighed. "Okay, what do I need to wear?"

I pulled out her outfit, and she changed quickly and haphazardly. Thankfully, someone had left a golf cart outside of our trailer that morning, so I confiscated it as we raced to set.

"They are going to fucking kill me," I sighed under my breath. "I'm going to be fucking fired."

"No, you won't," Spencer reassured me. "It'll be okay. Just let me speak to them."

She reached out and put her hand on my thigh to comfort me, but it had just the opposite effect. Holy hell, I could have crashed the cart and flown to heaven on adrenaline from her touch.

When we finally reached the set, I was bombarded by a plethora of production assistants who wanted no less than my head on a steak.

"Where the hell have you been?" one asked. "Your only job is to get the talent to the set. Is that too difficult for you?"

"I'm sorry," I sighed, but as I opened my mouth to tell the truth, Spencer cut me off.

"Look, it was my fault," she explained. "I was out late last night and overslept. Don't blame Lauren—it was my fault."

I could see the production assistants squirm in their shoes. They couldn't exactly yell at Spencer, but they needed some sort of punching bag for their anger. "Well, did you even try waking her?" one asked me in a huff.

"Actually, she did. And I'd really prefer you didn't speak to her in that tone," Spencer snapped.

Something in her demeanor had changed. I'd never seen her fired up before, but suddenly the calm and cheerful tone she'd had all day turned cold. Stepping between the junior producer and myself, her back stiffened and her shoulders puffed up defensively.

With a tone barely louder than a whisper, she looked him dead in the eye with a piercing gaze. "I think you owe Lauren an apology."

The small group of assistants and producers shared confused looks. The comment clearly took them aback. It was probably the first time they'd ever been reprimanded for speaking down to the "day help."

I wasn't sure whether to be impressed or embarrassed for having been put on the spot. More than anything, I was trying desperately not to swoon over her sudden shift into protector. "It's alright, Spencer. Really."

"No, I want to hear them say it," she replied, standing her ground.

The main offender stepped forward, and mumbled an apology, a tone of embarrassment in his voice. Satisfied, Spencer backed down.

"See, not so difficult to be polite, is it? Look, I'm here now. Can we please get to work?"

He nodded, "Yeah, let's get started."

Turning back towards me, Spencer shot me a soft smile and a comforting wink. "All good?"

"Yeah, all good," I replied.

"Alright, well time to shoot, but I'll see you later, okay?"

"Break a leg," I smiled. I still wasn't sure what had just gone down, but whatever it was had shifted the energy on set.

They dragged Spencer off to makeup as I fell back into

the cart. I had just dodged the biggest bullet of my career thus far.

"Maybe you should just head home for the day," the head production assistant told me. "This is Ms. Wolf's last scene of the day. We can make sure she has a ride home. Plus, you look like you could use a nap."

I knew that comment was meant to be an insult, but I *was* exhausted. "Are you sure," I asked. "I don't mind staying around to help out."

"No, you have done enough already." He huffed the answer with such a disgruntled voice that I didn't even dare argue.

"Alright," I sighed.

I could use some rest. The last couple of days had kicked my ass. We spent well over twelve hours a day on set, significantly more than my college body was used to. So, I returned to the trailer and gathered my things and went home.

I was due for a very long nap.

10

When I woke up that evening, I realized that Spencer had simultaneously saved my job and my ass. I reached for my phone to see if she had contacted me, but alas I was greeted with a blank screen. I decided, in that moment, to be bold. She had put herself out on limb for me, and I wanted to reciprocate the favor.

I quickly drafted a text asking if she was free and sent it without hesitation. Within seconds, I received a message back: *'Yeah :) What are you up to?'*

'Not much. Just woke up from a nap. Do you think I could come over? I wanted to thank you for earlier.'

'Of course! Room 304.'

I threw on my clothes and raced to her hotel room before I had a second thought. On my way out of my apartment, I grabbed the nicest bottle of booze I owned, which wasn't saying much, but who could be mad at someone with alcohol in hand?

It took some convincing for the woman working the front desk to allow me upstairs, but once I showed her my set badge, she immediately agreed. It was amazing what a kind smile and a laminated id could get you.

I knocked on Spencer's door, and to my surprise she greeted me in a robe.

I had instant flashbacks to the day we first met. I would never forget how deeply I wanted to see beneath that fabric. I now knew her better, and had a level of friendship and care for her that I never would have imagined. That didn't stop my brain from wandering, though.

"Come on in," she smiled. She opened the door wider and motioned for me to follow her into the room. "How was your nap?"

"It was good—much needed. I haven't been getting the best sleep the past week."

"Working on set always takes it out of me too," she smiled in agreement. She looked down at the bottle in my hands and nodded towards it. "What is that? Did you come bearing presents?"

"I just wanted to thank you again for this afternoon. You didn't have to take the blame today. It was my fault, and I really appreciate you taking the heat."

"No problem," she shrugged. "Trust me, they are not going to get mad at me. It's no big deal. They didn't even bring it up again."

"Well, thank you," I handed her the bottle. "I know it's not very expensive, but it was the best I had."

"It is wonderful!" she exclaimed. "You don't know how much I need a drink. Do you want to pour us a glass while I get changed. I should probably put on some actual clothes. I wouldn't want to scare you away again."

"Again? What's that supposed to mean?" I asked, racking my brain for previous spooks.

"Oh," she smiled. "Just that last time I invited you up here, you all but bolted."

"I did not!" I insisted.

"You did too!" she laughed. She let out a dramatic sigh

and feigned an old Hollywood faint. "I was all stuffed full of pancakes and left high and dry, just a way too full girl in a hotel room all alone."

How was one person so DAMN adorable?

"I'm sorry. I'm sorry," I giggled. "I just have a hard time knowing what's a polite invite or if you actually wanted me to come up. I assumed you were just being considerate."

"I'm just teasing," she smiled. "But do know, I'm never polite. If I invite you up, it's because I want to spend time with you."

She winked as she turned around and made her way to the bathroom. I was partly sad to see her robe go, but I knew that I would never be able to concentrate if she kept it on. My mind was already wandering, and I hadn't even begun to drink yet.

I searched through her mini-fridge to find some mixers. We had a limited selection, but I could make it work. "Do you trust me?" I asked, calling through the door.

"Entirely!"

"Good. I can make a pretty good drink, but it won't be fancy." My poor college skills were finally coming in handy.

I used the glasses as makeshift shakers as I mixed the alcohol and whatever else I could find. By the time I was done, I had two delicious drinks that actually looked pretty professional. Maybe I was missing my true calling.

When Spencer returned, she was wearing the cutest oversized sweatshirt and a pair of what looked like boxers. It was nearly impossible for me to take my eyes off of her as she walked through the room. She jumped down on the bed and patted a spot next to her signaling for me to join. I grabbed our drinks and sat a safe distance from her.

We began to drink slowly and discuss work as usual. We talked about her upcoming scenes and some of the weirdos on set. The more we talked, the looser I became, and by our second round of drinks, we were both leaning back against the bed and growing more personal with each passing minute.

Spencer took a sip and ran her fingers through her hair in thought. "If you could do anything, work wise I mean, what would you do?"

I leaned back against the bed and thought for a moment. "I guess I would be a writer. That has always been a dream of mine—not that it'll happen anytime soon."

"Why not?" she asked, an inquisitive look on her face. She took another sip of her drink and leaned forward towards me.

"Well, honestly, I'm too poor. I've got student loans to pay off and no job on the horizon. I need to find some real work soon before I can even think about what I want to do. I just don't have the flexibility for it yet, you know?"

She nodded quietly, but I could tell she didn't understand. Why would she? It wasn't something she could relate to on any level. She probably had more money than she knew what to do with, and the last thing she could imagine was being a poor student with no clear path. She had been living her dreams for the past five years.

"How about you?" I asked. "It must feel strange to have accomplished so much so young. You are doing something that most people only dream about."

"Yeah, I guess," she nodded thoughtfully. "It was never my dream, though. At least, not like this. I never really wanted to be famous really. I know that must sound silly; who wants to get into acting but not be famous? It's the truth though. I hate the media attention. There is nothing worse than the promotions and photoshoots. It is all so vain. Sometimes I just feel like a hollow shell for other people."

"I guess I never thought about it like that," I admitted. "What would you do if you could do anything?"

"I guess I would work on lower budget things—projects that mattered to me. Not that it'll happen anytime soon; not full-time at least. Those are good side projects. My management would never let me do them more than for the 'critical acclaim.'"

"So, the films you've worked on haven't really mattered to you?"

"Not really," she sighed. "I just want some sort of control over my work. I'm just a mouthpiece at the moment. I guess that would be my ultimate dream: to make the decisions one day."

"You are so much different than I thought you were going to be," I replied, taking another sip of my drink. The alcohol was hitting me quickly, and I could find myself saying things I normally wouldn't have.

"What do you mean by that?" she asked.

"I guess I just thought you would be—"

"Stupid?" she cut me off.

"No, not stupid. Hard to get to know."

"So you heard the rumors around set before you met me," Spencer chuckled. "Everyone else seems to think I am a grade-A bitch. Someone told me once that I was 'hard to work with,' though I don't really understand why."

"Yeah," I admitted. "I heard a few things. I knew not to believe them though."

"Do you think I'm hard to work with?" There was suddenly concern in her voice.

"Not at all. I think you don't seem to fit in with the others, though, so I can see why they may take that out on you."

"I get nervous," she whispered. "It is so much harder for me to open up to the others. I know it comes across poorly, but I don't know how to fix it."

"You didn't have a problem opening up to me?" I asked.

"No, not at all. You are different than I thought you would be as well. I knew I was going to like you from the moment I met you. I just didn't realize how much I was going to like you."

"Yeah?"

"Yeah. I like you more than I've liked anyone in a long time."

I felt my stomach begin to churn with nerves. Taking another sip of my drink, I replied, "I like you more than I've liked anyone in a long time too."

She reached out her hand and touched my leg softly. "Enough to let me kiss you?"

I didn't know what to say. My whole body felt on fire. It was as if my brain just got up and left, leaving me utterly without thought.

I heard the soft yes before I realized I had said it.

Spencer leaned forward and closed the gap between us. She brought her hand up from my leg to my cheek. She moved toward me slowly. It was as if I was watching a scene from the outside.

Her soft, pink lips approached, and all at once we were kissing. It was gentle at first, soft in a way I hadn't imagined. This was my first time actually kissing another woman, and it felt so right, so normal.

I leaned my body into her and loosened my tense muscles. I relaxed. Our lips moved together as we explored one another. It was as if I had waited the last two weeks to do just this.

Spencer shifted on the bed, moving up closer to the pillows. "Come here," she whispered, taking my hand and pulling me towards her. I set down our drinks and followed her lead. She was entirely in charge, and that was hot as hell.

As I moved up towards the head of the bed, Spencer

positioned me so that we were laying side by side. We stared at each other for a moment, taking in one another for the first time. Her eyes were a soft hazel green, and they sparkled in a way I hadn't noticed before.

She was even more beautiful up close if that was even possible.

Spencer wrapped her arm around my waist and kissed me again, this time less tenderly and more desperately. Her tongue parted my lips and found its counterpart in my mouth. We moved into one another, and she held me close as we made out.

I felt like a teenager again.

We stayed wrapped in each other's arms for what felt like hours. I was so tired and so hungry for affection that this simple embrace felt like heaven. I didn't realize how much I had wanted Spencer until I had her. It had been so long since I felt anything real for another person that I was shocked by the intensity of it. Perhaps I had never actually felt this level of attraction, it took me so by surprise.

Kissing was so simple, so innocent, yet it felt life changing. We rolled around on the bed, arms tangled together, exploring one another as if we had never kissed before. In that moment, it didn't matter that Spencer was an actress or that I was her assistant. All that matter was that we fit perfectly into one another.

I didn't want to go to sleep. I didn't want this moment to end, but my eyes betrayed me. I tried so hard to fight the fatigue, but it overwhelmed me. All at once, my eyes shut and I fell asleep in Spencer's arms.

11

I WOKE the next morning to the sound of soft snoring. It took me a moment to adjust to my surroundings, but the realization of my location hit me like a ton of bricks.

Turning my head slightly, I opened my groggy eyes and saw Spencer laying inches from my face. I had found the source of the adorable snores.

Ring! Ring!

Sitting up, I saw that Spencer's phone was dancing on the bedside table with the vibrations of an incoming call. I reached out my hand and lightly touched her back, hoping she might stir, but she merely rolled over with a groan.

"Spencer," I whispered, rubbing her back slightly harder this time. "Spencer, your phone is ringing."

"Hmm?" she murmured.

"Your phone," I replied. Reaching out, I grabbed the device and placed it in front of her tired eyes until she woke fully.

When her eyes fully opened, she sat up in bed and answered the phone. Her hair was slightly untamed, but otherwise she looked as if she had just stepped off a photoshoot.

How did she manage to look so damn hot all the time?

"Hello?" she said groggily. There was a pause and a look of horror flashed over her face. "Oh, shit! I'm so sorry!"

I sat up in the bed and watched with curiosity as she answered the call. I could see she was anxious even without hearing the other end of the call, but I couldn't piece together the reason for her distress. The set was closed for the day, so whatever happened must not have been related to the film.

"No, I totally forgot to set my alarm" Spencer continued. "Look, Rebecca, I am leaving right now. I'll get on the next plane. It'll be okay. Just tell them I got held up a few hours."

Ending the phone call, Spencer turned to me with a look of exhaustion in her eyes. "Can I ask you the biggest favor? Is there any way you could drive me to the airport? If not, I can call a car, but I would much prefer you."

"Of course!" I replied. "What's going on? Is everything okay?"

"Yeah, I just completely forgot to set my alarm last night, so I missed my flight. Hopefully they will have another sometime this afternoon." She jumped out of bed and began throwing clothes from across the room into a small suitcase.

"Oh," I replied, completely taken aback. "Are you going somewhere?"

"Yeah, I've got to do a press junket for a movie that's coming out next month. Did nobody tell you I would be gone?" She took a short break from her hasty packing to shoot me an inquisitive glance.

"No, I had no idea," I shrugged.

I was trying my best to act nonchalant about the whole thing, but it was difficult not to feel a little strange. We had just made out all night, and not only were neither of us addressing the issue, but Spencer was fleeing the state. I didn't want to be clingy, but I couldn't help the sad shooting pains reverberating around my chest.

"That's weird. Someone should have told you. I'm going to talk to Rebecca about making sure you're included in my full schedule during shooting," she sighed as she started frantically tossing clothes into a suitcase. "Well, I have to fly back to LA for the next five days. I'm sorry I didn't think to tell you, but thankfully it is less than a week. Plus, it means you get a break from set as well. I'm sure you need it by now."

"I do," I nodded in agreement.

Spencer continued to pack her bag while we sat in silence. Last night had been so good, but I was suddenly questioning whether it had meant more to me than it had to her. She hadn't even addressed it, and that made me more insecure than anything.

The ride to the airport was uncomfortable to say the least. It wasn't a very far drive, but Spencer was so caught up in making flight arrangements that our conversation dwindled. I wanted so badly to ask her what the previous night had meant, but she was absorbed in her work and I was a coward.

When we finally reached the departure gate, I pulled up to the drop-off area and turned to Spencer. She was still nose deep in her phone, so I tried to clear my throat in an attempt to signal her. Glancing up, she realized where we were and snapped out of her stupor.

"Oh, are we here already?" Spencer asked with a disappointed tone.

"Yeah, it didn't take as long as I thought," I shrugged. I didn't want to her to know the truth: I felt every minute in my bones.

"Shit," she sighed. "The last thing I want right now is to go back to LA"

She leaned forward and rifled through her bag until she found a pair of oversized sunglasses and a beanie. Slipping them on, she became an entirely new person behind her mask. It was amazing to see the lengths she went to not to be noticed in public.

"It is only a week, right?" I shrugged, trying to justify the time apart more for myself than Spencer.

"Only a week," she repeated. She glanced down at her watch begrudgingly and nodded, "Well, I guess I should go. I booked a flight, and I need to check in."

There was a hesitation. I didn't quite know what to say. Was I supposed to kiss her goodbye or was last night a one-off situation?

"I guess I will see you in a week, then," I sighed. It was the best I could come up with in the moment.

"I guess so," she sighed.

Collecting her bags in her hand, she reached for the door handle before hesitating. On second thought, she turned towards me and kissed me softly on each side of my face. It was a simple kiss goodbye, but her lips lingered just a moment longer, as if they knew they were in familiar territory.

With that, she opened the door and stepped out of the car. I watched as she walked to the outdoor check-in stand. I watched as she smiled and took pictures with the baggage handlers. I watched as she turned around and waved just one last time, and, finally, I watched as she walked inside the airport and disappeared behind the frosted glass.

The ride back to my apartment was somehow even more hollow than the ride there. My car felt like an overinflated balloon, and I felt very alone. No matter how much I tried to shut off my mind, I couldn't stop analyzing the past 12 hours. Spencer and I had kissed the night before, hadn't we? Was it all just a dream? I had been thinking about her so much lately that perhaps my mind had fabricated the entire thing.

I didn't understand.

I wished I had asked her while she was still trapped in my car. I wish I had built up the courage. I just wasn't that person. I had left this gaping question mark in my mind, and now the insecurities were beginning to flood in.

Perhaps it had meant nothing to Spencer. She was, after all beautiful and famous. She probably had flocks of people lined up for her every night. Perhaps I was just a blip on her radar: someone totally inconsequential.

I tried to convince myself of that but I just couldn't. There was a tenderness in her touch that I couldn't imagine was easily faked. It wasn't as if I was just a one night stand. We hadn't even had sex. We spent the entire night just fucking kissing.

Who does that?

When I finally got back to my apartment, I made a beeline back to my bedroom hoping to remain unseen. Unfortunately, I caught the attention of my roommate, Allie.

"Lauren! Where were you? We were starting to get worried!" she called from the kitchen.

Poking her head out into the hallway, she smiled to greet me. Her smiled quickly faded to confusion, however, as she glanced down at my clothes. I was wearing the same outfit as yesterday, only significantly more wrinkled. I had never been known to indulge in a one-night stand, mostly because I hated everyone, so I could see why Allie was confused.

"Where have you been? Were you with someone?" Her eyebrows twisted as they tried to solve the mystery.

"No," I sighed. I tried my best to act as inconspicuously as possible. "I mean, I was with Spencer, but we were working. It got late, so I just decided to crash."

"Oh," Allie looked visibly surprised. "You must really be enjoying work, then."

"I am," I nodded. "I need a break though. Thankfully I am off next week."

"Are they done filming already? That seems quick."

"No, we still have a few weeks to go, but Spencer has to go back to LA for a press tour. She's promoting her new movie, so I don't have to go to set."

"It is so weird hearing you call her by her first name," Allie shook her head. "It's cool, don't get me wrong, but so strange. You and her seem to have gotten pretty close lately."

She didn't know the half of it. "Yeah, well I think I should go to bed. It was a long night."

"Oh, of course," she smiled, turning back to her cereal. I could tell there was still a hint of doubt in her mind, but I wasn't going to push the issue out of fear that it might push back.

12

THE NEXT FEW days dragged by painfully slowly. I kept waiting for Spencer to text or call or reach out in some way, but all I heard was radio silence. It was a strange feeling, sitting around and waiting for someone to call. It wasn't an action I had ever experienced before. I guess I had just never cared enough about anyone else.

I knew she was busy. The weirdest part of the whole situation was that anytime I turned on the news or walked by my roommates on their computers, I caught glimpses of her. There were articles and interviews that bombarded me at every corner.

It was as if she existed in two separate worlds. It was almost painful for me to see her on all these platforms when all I wanted was to ask her about her day. She had become such a part of my routine the past month that not talking to her for a week was strange.

I made it halfway through my week off before my room-mates began to grow concerned about my utter lack of movement from the apartment. It wasn't until Allie caught me ordering my second pizza of the week that she decided something needed to be done. She all but planned an intervention.

"We need to get out of this apartment," she declared. "Come on, let's go do something fun! Anything!"

"Like what?" I asked, my mouth half full with stuffed crust cheese.

"How about we go to the movies?" I could tell she had been working up to that answer for a while. Allie was many things, but subtle was not one of them.

"We never go to the movies," I replied.

"I know, but it's different now. With them filming at the university, I have a new respect for the art of it all."

"Yeah, right," I huffed.

"I am also dying to see the new Spencer Wolf movie."

"Ding, ding, ding! Now we have the true answer!" I teased. "No."

"Oh, come on! You know you want to as well! Have you ever actually seen a movie she's been in?"

"I guess not," I shrugged, racking my brain.

"Please," she pleaded. "You two are basically friends now. Wouldn't it be so cool to see her up on the movie screen?"

"I don't know." I honestly couldn't tell if I would find it fascinating or horrifying.

"Please," she continued. "Do it for me. She and I are now basically friends once removed. I'll even pay for your movie ticket." She folded her hands in a faux prayer position.

I glanced around my room. I hadn't left the apartment in three days, and I needed to get out. Half of me did want to see Spencer, even fake Spencer, enough that I would put up with watching her in some Hollywood love story.

"Fine," I agreed. "But, you are buying me a large popcorn as well."

"Deal!" Allie squealed. "I already checked the movie times. If we get ready now, we can make the midday show."

"Alright," I sighed. "Let me put on some real pants."

By the time we got to the movie theater, I was already questioning my decision. Would Spencer even want me to watch her work? Did I care? She was the one off promoting the thing, so why should I deprive myself of the entertainment. Half of me wanted to text her and tell her I was watching it, but there was no way that wasn't weird.

I could feel the butterflies in my stomach as we sat in the theater and waited for the opening credits to roll. I didn't know why, but I felt like I was seeing her again in person for the first time. It was as if I was meeting a totally different side of her, and it terrified me.

My heart nearly stopped the first time I saw her on screen. It was all so surreal, so entirely strange watching a person I had touched in the flesh up on the big screen. She was a good actress, I would give her that; Allie was crying within the first thirty minutes. The experience was far less enjoyable for me, however.

It was, after all, a romance movie, and I couldn't help but resent the male lead for his role. I knew he was just acting, but every time they kissed or showed any sign of affection, I felt a pang in my heart that I couldn't quite explain. My stomach churned when I watched them roll around in bed together. I couldn't believe I was jealous of a fucking movie character.

The whole process was strange in a way that I didn't quite enjoy. Perhaps I could have relaxed into it more if Spencer and I hadn't left on such odd terms, but it just made me more self-conscious of us as I watched her fall in love with this other person. I knew it was fake, but it was like watching a video of her and I when they kissed. I couldn't help but think of those lips on me.

When the final credits rolled, I breathed a sigh of relief and realized I had been tense the entire movie. Allie, on the other hand, couldn't stop gushing. Everything that I hated about it had struck a chord with her, and I had to endure a car ride home listening to her gush about the chemistry between the two actors.

I wanted so desperately to grab her and shake her, tell her all about Spencer and I and our night in bed together, but I couldn't. I didn't want to let her in on my little secret. Even if it pained me, it was all mine.

———

THE FOLLOWING few days were even more boring. I tried my best to keep Spencer off my mind, but she was everywhere. From billboards to advertisements online, she popped up no matter what I did.

It didn't help that my own mind was a constant stream of her.

In my dreams, she kissed me again in the hotel, and when I woke my body still ached for her. I needed something, anything, to help me feel relief.

One of the most confusing yet simultaneously easy parts of the whole situation was the question mark Spencer presented in terms of my sexuality.

I'd always known that I liked women too, but I had only had one other relationship before: a boy from my program who had wanted more commitment after a year of dating than I was willing to give.

I had liked him—at least I thought I had—but nothing I ever felt for him compared to what I was feeling right now. I had never truly questioned myself before. More than anything, I never really thought much about sex, at least not the hetero-sex with which I was acquainted.

Now, I couldn't get simple kissing off my mind.

Was it possible that'd I was a hell of a lot more gay than I realized?

For a long period of my life, I wondered if there was something wrong with me. I never went through the boy-crazed adolescent period which seemed to plague other girls. I never developed playground crushes on my male friends. I never went through the same process that all my peers seemed to undertake. For years, I had just passed off that indifference as being around immature boys, but now I began to wonder if there was something else at play all along.

It didn't matter in the end. Things with Spencer were going nowhere fast. I had all but convinced myself over the past few days that whatever happened was merely drunken fun for her. Why would someone like her care about someone like me? Besides, even if she did like me, what future could we have? She would be leaving again soon after production ended, and I would remain here with nothing but memories of someone I would likely see in the news weekly.

By the time Wednesday rolled around, I tried my hardest to act cool. Rebecca had emailed me Spencer's weekly itinerary, so I knew she was arriving in the city mid-day at our small airport. I figured she could text me if she wanted. I didn't have the nerve to make the first move, not after a week of talking myself out of our relationship.

That didn't stop me, however, from waiting by my phone in anticipation. The hours ticked by and my patience wore thin until, finally, my phone chirped to life in the early evening hours. It was Spencer.

'Hey you,' she typed.

'Hey,' I wrote back.

After not hearing from her all week, I was a bit surprised

by how casual she was being. Maybe she really hadn't been thinking about me all week like I had been thinking of her. That was a surprisingly painful thought, so I tried my best to shake it out of my head and match her level of calm tone.

'*What are you up to?*' she wrote back immediately.

'*Not much, what about you?*'

'*I just woke up from the longest nap. I'm at my hotel. So exhausted, it's crazy! Would you mind coming over? There is something I wanted to talk to you about.*'

There it was. I knew it was coming, but I was glad she got straight to the point. She was going to fire me or tell me the other night had been a mistake, I was sure of it.

'*Sure, I can be there in 30 minutes.*'

13

———

THE FEW MILES to the hotel were the most nerve-wracking drive I had ever taken. My hands were shaking so much that I worried I might not be able to hold the steering wheel.

When I finally reached the front entrance, I took a deep breath and went inside.

To my surprise, she greeted me wearing loose running pants and a ratty old t-shirt. She looked so unlike the person I had seen all over TV the past few days that it was almost shocking.

"Hey," she smiled, reaching out to hug me deeply. I wondered if she could see just how nervous I was. We hugged for just a moment longer than necessary, and I had to resist the urge to melt into her. "Come on in."

We stepped inside her hotel room, but I didn't sit down. The last thing I wanted was to make this any more awkward than it had to be. If we were going to rip the bandaid off, we might as well rip it quickly.

"So, what was it you wanted to talk to me about?" I asked, leaning against the wall.

She took a deep breath and sat on the edge of the bed. "Wow, we are really getting straight to it, aren't we?"

"Why not, right?" I shrugged. I could feel my defensive bristles raising in preparation.

"Did you have a good week, at least?"

"Not really," I admitted. "It was very...long."

She nodded in understanding. "Mine was pretty long as well. Press junkets are normally long and exhausting, but this one was even worse than usual. It was worse because I couldn't wait to get back here."

My ears perked up. "Why back here?"

"Because I couldn't stop thinking about you. We left on a weird note, a bad note, and it has bothered me all week. I don't want you to think that I kissed you because I was bored or that it meant nothing to me. I thought about you every single second of every day. I was so caught up in this world of fake people, and all I wanted was you."

"Why didn't you text or call?" I asked.

"Why didn't you?"

Spencer leaned forward in the bed until she was practically falling off. "Look, Lauren, I want you. I want to be with you. Not just as some work thing, not just as a set romance, but as something...more. I don't know how we can make it work just yet, but I am willing to give it a try. We can figure the rest out later. That is, if you are interested."

I took a deep breath and tried to steady my nerves. This was the last thing I thought might happen this evening. Glancing back up into her eyes, I saw a pleading, almost desperate look.

"I don't really know what I want," I admitted. "I've thought about you every moment since you left. About our kiss. About the way you felt on top of me. I don't know what that means, but I like it. I like being with you. I like being around you."

"That's all I need."

A soft smile spread over Spencer's lips. She stood up and crossed the room in three long strides.

With a soft push against my stomach, she threw me back against the wall.

Her hand reached up and tangled itself in the hair at the base of my neck, and she kissed me deeply. If she hadn't been there to brace my body, I think my knees would have given out.

We moved into one another. Arms and lips and tongues molded together until we felt like one body. Just as I was falling head over heels into her, she pulled away quickly and looked me in the eye.

"Is this what you want?" she whispered, her thumbs tracing the outline of my lip.

"Yes," I whispered.

She was so fucking beautiful.

I grabbed her face and pulled her back into me. I didn't need to overthink it any longer. I just needed her.

As we kissed, she reached out and kicked apart my legs, spreading me wider. She stepped into the gap, pushed her hips up against mine and ground into me as if we were at a middle school dance.

I thought I might die of happiness.

She moved against my body as if she were molded for me, pressing every inch of herself against me. God, she felt so good. Her hands moved down my throat and to my stomach, and her mouth followed, leaving bites and nibbles all the way. I couldn't suppress the moan that escaped my lips, but it only seemed to spur her further.

Before I knew what was happening, we were fumbling at each other's clothes, tearing them piece by piece from our bodies. She pulled my shirt over my head. My hands moved up inside hers, and I slid it off in one motion. We worked on each other's bras with quaking fingers, and it was obvious we were both nervous.

When we finally freed the hooks, the two flimsy pieces of fabric were tossed out of the way. Her breasts were absolutely breathtaking. Her perfectly symmetrical nipples as hard as could be. They were as pink as her rosy cheeks and firm beyond belief.

We grabbed each other, touched each other, massaged each other. Finally her lips found my way down to my aching nipples. The feel of her mouth against my chest drove me absolutely insane. It took every ounce of my effort not to pin her down and never let her go.

Before I could reciprocate, Spencer wrapped her arms around my waist and lifted me ease. I was impressed. I knew she was strong, but I'd never had someone pick me up before. She carried me to the bed and threw me down against the soft mattress. My heart leapt in my chest as she looked down at me, took in every inch of my exposed skin and smiled.

I was her's, all her's.

Climbing between my legs, she began to trace her lips down my midsection. Her fingers fumbled to undo my jeans. She pulled the tight fabric, and we giggled when it took her a full four tries just to get them off. I had never giggled during sex before, let alone wanted someone so badly, and I was soaking in every second of it.

I tried to sit up to meet her, but she pushed me back against the bed. "Stay down," she instructed. "Let me handle the rest."

Tossing my jeans across the room, there was now just one layer between me and her, and I wanted it so desperately to disappear from my body. She teased me, kissing my inner thigh and biting my skin, before finally wrapping a finger inside the waistband of the flimsy fabric around my hips.

"Is this what you want?" she asked again.

"Yes, please," the words came out more in a moan than in a reply.

She slipped one finger inside and traced her way down the sides of my opening. Her touch felt electric.

"My god, you are beautiful," she whispered. She looked down at me from above, her lips so pink I wanted to bite them.

"Kiss me," I begged. "Please."

She leaned down and met my lips with hers, her fingers still working their magic between my legs.

I was throbbing.

I was on fire.

I needed her desperately.

As she kissed me, I let my hands roam down her body until I found the waistband of her running shorts. When I slipped my hand inside, I realized with surprise that she wasn't wearing anything underneath. She was warm, warmer than I had expected, and my fingers couldn't wait to explore every inch of her.

We began to touch each other simultaneously, explore each other in the most intimate way. When her arms finally tired, she rolled over and we laid side by side.

Our fingers quickly resumed their search. We moved into one another simultaneously, and our lips danced in desire. My whole body was tingling with pleasure. I was so pent up, so in need of release, but I wanted this moment to last. I held off my climax for as long as I could, but I knew the moment was coming, and I knew it was coming fast.

Spencer must have sensed that I was close. Her fingers quicken their pace, and I felt an ache begin to spread from my toes up to my thighs. I felt a moan vibrate in my chest.

My stomach tightened in anticipation, and all at once my whole body spasmed in orgasmic bliss.

My weight collapsed in Spencer's arms, and she held me tight as I regained my composure. It was the most intense orgasm of my life, and my body could hardly handle the energy that flowed from my toes all the way through my fingertips.

I was in heaven.

After a deep breath, I returned my attention to Spencer. The intensity of my orgasm only made me want to please her more. Sliding my finger over her, I felt her moan in pleasure. She leaned in and kissed me deeply as I continued to write circled between her thighs.

I could feel Spencer respond to my touch, and giving her that pleasure was the hottest thing I had ever done. Her arm tightened around my waist, pulling me closer to her, and her kiss became harder and more desperate.

She was close, but I was enjoying this too much to let her finish quickly. Instead, I drew out the moment, teasing her with the pace of my touch and making her all but beg for relief.

Finally, after I had tortured her enough, I sped up my finger and kissed her with all the passion I could muster. With a deep sigh, her body shuddered into me and Spencer came. I had never seen anything more beautiful than the look on her face in that moment.

Falling back against the pillow, Spencer took a deep breath and began to giggle happily. "Do you know how many times I've thought about that the past week?" she asked.

I couldn't help but smile knowing she had thought about me after all. "And here I thought you would forget all about me as soon as you got back to LA."

"I don't think I could ever forget about those lips," she

replied. Her index finger traced a line around my mouth as she stared, taking me in.

Reaching up, she brushed a strand of hair away from my face. I tried my best to stifle a yawn, but the urge was too powerful to resist. I laid my head down next to her's on the pillow and felt exhaustion sweep through my body. Spencer had worn me out.

Before I knew it, my eyes gave into temptation, and I fell deeply into a heavy slumber. For the first time in a long while, the reality of the night was better than anything I could have dreamed.

I still wasn't quite sure what would happen in the coming weeks when Spencer finished filming. I still wasn't quite sure what this meant about for my sexuality or my future in this small, college town. The only thing I knew for certain was that I wanted Spencer, and Spencer wanted me.

For now, that was enough.

14

I woke up the next morning the soft glow of sunlight trickling in through the curtains. Stretching my arms, I basked in the wonderfully sore muscles aching throughout my body. Last night had been everything and more.

Rolling over, my heart fluttered when I saw the adorably ruffled hair of Spencer still lying on the pillow next to me. Her face was soft and peacefully asleep, and I couldn't help but admire the way the sunlight shown down over her perfect skin.

She was gorgeous, and I was in her bed.

How in the hell had I ended up here? How had I gotten so lucky?

What would me from a month ago say about where I found myself this morning?

With a soft smile, her eyes flutter open slowly. Her grin turned into a full-on smile as realization washed over her face.

"Well, hello there darling," Spencer cooed.

I couldn't believe how adorable she was.

"Well, hello sleepy head," I smiled back.

She rolled over across the bed and into my arms as she

planted a kiss on my lips. It felt so natural, so second nature. Blissfully normal.

If I didn't know any better, I would think I was still dreaming.

Just as we were sliding back into each other's arms again, a sharp rap on the door pulled us apart like a lightning bolt. I could feel myself jump back in bed afraid that we'd been caught, but Spencer just smiled and shrugged it off.

"Don't worry babe," she said, brushing the hair from my startled face. "That should just be the room service I ordered last night."

I could feel my eyebrows raise in anticipation.

"Oh, room service, huh?" I asked. "When did you order that?"

Spencer shrugged and a blush seemed to creep over her cheeks, "Oh, before you got here."

"Before I got here? And how did you guess I'd be staying?" I teased, enjoying the pink twinge still visible on her cheeks.

Seeming to dodge the question, she rolled out of bed, grabbed a robe from the chair in the corner and made her way to the door. Answering it, I could hear her make friendly small talk with the bellhop as she insisted that she could bring in the food herself.

I sat up in bed and watched with humor as world-famous-actress, Spencer Wolf, rolled in an entire cart full of food doing her best server role-play. It looked like she had ordered the whole menu.

"How much food did you get?!" I asked watching in disbelief as she lifted lid after lid from the room service trays.

"Well, I thought we just might be a little bit hungry," she replied the blush creepy and even further up her cheeks.

Something about seeing her nervous made her even

more endearing. If that was at all possible.

I decided to play into it a little bit, given that this was the first time our roles had seemingly shifted. And I was having fun.

"So, you went ahead and ordered breakfast for us? Now that was a little presumptuous, wasn't it, Miss Wolf?"

"You call it presumptuous. But I prefer hopeful." And just like that, she'd taken charge once again

Arranging the food on the small dining table in her luxurious suite, Spencer shot me a wink. "Now, would you like to interrogate me more on my intentions from last night, or would you like to join me some for some breakfast Miss Daly?"

God, how was she so sexy? I had a feeling I was gonna get used to this.

Slipping out of bed, I was suddenly self-conscious for the first time, realizing that one of the fittest women in the world was across the room eyeing me, naked and entirely vulnerable. It wasn't like I did this very often. In fact, I've never really let anyone see me exposed like this, but her eyes were glued to me as I quickly trotted across the room and to the bathroom to grab the second robe.

"Hey," she whispered. "Let me look at you as you move. Don't I get to enjoy the show?"

"I'm just not really used to this," I whispered. "I'm not really used to being naked around anyone else. Not like you. I mean, Lordy, you're naked for shoots all the time I'm sure."

Spencer gave me a quizzical look, but smiled as she walked across the room and cupped my slightly embarrassed face in her hand. "I guess," she nodded."I don't really think about it like that, though. I mean, yeah, a lot of people probably do see me naked. But not like this. Not like the way I want you to see me."

I didn't realize that butterflies could jump so high in my

stomach.

"It might just take me some time to get used to it," I confessed. "I want to though."

"Good," she smiled planting a kiss on my lips. "Now, let's dig in before the food gets cold."

She didn't have to ask me twice. I was starving. Who knew that sex with a beautiful woman could take so much energy out of you? If we kept this up I was gonna have six-pack abs by the end of the month.

Taking my hand, she led me to the table, pulled out the chair, and offered me a seat. Who knew that Spencer Wolf was this chivalrous? She really did have that top-daddy energy that I pegged the first day we met.

As we passed around the numerous plates of over-flowing food, we made the sort of simple, breakfast small-talk that I had always dreamed of having with a partner. It was lovely, sitting here with her plotting out our days together in comfortable ease. And I couldn't help but wonder what that made us? I mean, our relationship had changed entirely last night, but was I being naïve to think that there might be more?

Mustering all the gumption I had in my body, I decided the best course of action would be to just tackle it head-on.

Mama didn't raise no side-stepping bitch.

"So," I started, nerves threatening to take over my voice. "About last night..."

Spencer nodded slowly set her fork down on her plate and looked up. I tried to gauge the look in her eye. What was it? Confusion, concern, uncertainty?

"Yeah... I guess we should talk about it shouldn't we?"

"Yeah, I have to admit I wasn't expecting any of that to happen," I confessed. "I mean, don't get me wrong! I loved every second of it. And... If I'm being honest I would really like to do it again."

Spencer looked up at me and a smile tugged at her lips. I could feel my heart racing through my chest as she took a moment to respond, seemingly thinking as she took me in.

"Well, of course I want to do it again." she finally replied with a flirtatious lilt. "I never would have invited you here in the first place if I didn't wanna make this something more."

Relief seeped through my body. I could feel a smile spread across my own face, matching hers.

"But," she continued. "I do think we should talk about how we approach it."

Spencer sat back in her chair and took a deep sigh. "I guess we should talk about the fact that this isn't a normal relationship. It just can't be. I don't live a normal life. And everything we do and I do - it's all under scrutiny. And, there's the fact that, you know...I'm not out. At least, not publicly."

I set my fork down and felt a deep sigh roll through my chest as my nerves hit me once again. I hadn't even thought about all that. "So, yeah, you're still publicly in the closet...I hadn't really thought about that until now."

"It's... not that I'm not out. Rebecca knows. And she even knows about you. It was admittedly pretty hard for me to stop talking about you when I was in LA. Apparently, my poker face isn't that good," Spencer replied, reaching across the table to take my hand.

"So, what does that mean for us?" I asked, playing with the fingers she had laced between my own.

"Well, I know what it means for me. It means that I wanna keep seeing you. Desperately. If you'll have me. But, we're gonna have to be quiet about it, at least for now."

I nodded, letting the information sink in. It made sense, I mean her career was at stake here. And she'd never been confirmed to be with anyone serious, at least not publicly.

"I do wanna keep seeing you too." I leaned forward

assuring her reaching my hand across the table to take hers. "So, I guess that means we just have to be careful?"

Spencer smiled, and I could see relief wash across her face. She took my hand and brought it up to her lips, kissing my knuckles, each and every one. "Yes. Careful. But, that also means that we have my entire hotel room and the trailer to be ourselves. We just might have to be careful on set."

I nodded in agreement, the skin on my hand still tingling from her gorgeous lips. "We can absolutely be careful. I'll try and keep my hands off you, I promise."

"And I promise you nothing of the sort. When we're alone, expect my hands to be all over you."

I giggled nervously. She was so forward, and I couldn't believe this was happening to me. "Is that so?"

"Mmhmm," she hummed, taking another sip of her drink. "I am so very curious about you, Lauren. What you taste like. What makes you moan. Where you like to be touched. How long I can take you just on the edge. I want to discover all of it and so much more. I like you, if you couldn't already tell."

Oh my god, I thought to myself. Am I about to have a heart attack? Or an aneurysm? My chest felt tight and I couldn't swallow, I was so parched.

"I like you too," I replied with a soft smile.

"Good," she laughed. A mischievous glint flashed through her eyes. "On that note, I just got the notification that we're switching to night-shoots tonight. That means we have a whole day to waste. Whatdaya say we make the most of it?"

"That sounds absolutely amazing."

And, just like that, the food was momentarily forgotten as Spencer pulled me right back to bed.

15

LATER THAT AFTERNOON, after a second and third round of food and fun in bed, Spencer and I finally pulled ourselves out of the hotel room and to the waiting car down below to take us to set for her night shoot.

After such an intimate 24 hours, I had to admit that it felt odd to re-join the outside world. We'd had such a wonderful time in our little bubble, that it was difficult to slip my hand from Spencer's the moment we exited the hotel door.

I knew she was right. We had to be careful.

But, *even still*, my hand felt cold the second she released it out in the wild.

Spencer must've felt my mood change, because as we slipped into the backseat of the waiting town car, she gave me one last, final hand squeeze before turning her attention to the wandering eyes of the driver.

It didn't take long to arrive on set, but I spent the entire ride hyper aware of Spencer sitting next to me. She was so close. Close enough that I could feel the heat radiating off of her body. And yet, we weren't alone.

No matter how much I wanted to reach over and close the gap between us, we had to remain feet apart.

This was going to be harder than I expected.

———

IT WAS as if the air had been sucked from the car the moment we stepped out and into the waiting crowd of PAs and crew gathered at the set entrance.

I could hardly breathe.

The private bubble of Spencer and I had burst.

Rebecca swooped in fast and caffeinated. She pulled Spencer by the elbow into the chaos as I felt alone again standing in the sidelines.

Rebecca and Spencer talked easily, their conversation floating above the thick layer of tension that filled the set.

Spencer seemed so at ease. So collected. So nonchalant.

As if the past 24 hours had not just happened.

The woman had rocked my entire world, and she was acting like we'd just had a normal weekend.

My emotions were swirling.

Was this how things would be?

"So, you have a good couple days off, Lauren?" Rebecca asked as we stood to the side waiting for Spencer as she got her nose powdered.

I nodded, not trusting my voice not to crack. "Oh, yeah. It was really great to sleep in and have a little bit of a break. How was LA?"

"Busy," she sighed. "LA is always busy. There is always someone needing something from someone."

"Sounds stressful," I commiserated.

"It is." Rebecca leaned in close and lowered her voice. "You have to be careful here. There are eyes everywhere. It's hard. Especially in a town like LA."

I didn't know how to respond. Luckily, Rebecca continued, saving me from answering.

"Look, just be careful, okay? This business is cut-throat. People are always looking for their next story. Always. The media, the fans, the paparazzi. You can't trust anyone, not even the people you work with."

"I didn't really think about that," I admitted.

"Yeah, I didn't either, and it almost got me into a lot of trouble a few years ago. So, just watch your step, and if you're ever unsure, come find me, okay?"

I couldn't imagine being in this position, and I couldn't fathom the thought that someone might be watching us, waiting for us to slip up and become the story.

I suddenly felt my chest tighten with anxiety. Did Rebecca know about Spencer and I? Did it matter if she did? Her job was to protect Spencer, after all. She must have some idea that we had taken the next step in our flirtations.

But, then why would she not have mentioned anything about it.

She probably thought I was silly.

A little nobody from a small, insignificant town.

A girl who had no idea what it was like to be in the spotlight.

Maybe she was right.

"Lauren?"

Rebecca's voice pulled me from my self-deprecation. "Yeah?"

"Are you alright?"

"I'm fine," I replied. "Just trying to wrap my head around everything. There's a lot to think about. I just never imagined this would be my life, you know?"

"I do," she nodded. "And, that's why I'm telling you to be careful. You've caught Spencer's eye, and that's a pretty big deal. But, you're right. This is a lot. And, if you need anything, or you're having second thoughts, please don't hesitate to come and find me, okay?"

"Okay."

"Great," she said with a smile. "We don't want another situation like Jen.

"Jen?" I asked. That was a name I'd not heard before, and the way Rebecca whispered it made me feel like I was missing some secret backstory.

"Jen was Spencer's girlfriend about a year ago. She was a model and a pretty up-and-coming face in the industry. She and Spencer were together for about 6 months before everything went down."

"What happened?" I asked, curious. My heart was racing thinking about Spencer with someone else.

"Well, it all started out pretty innocently. They met on a shoot, and hit it off. Jen was sweet and funny, and she and Spencer became fast friends. After a few weeks, they started dating, and it was all good. But, the longer they were together, the more Jen wanted her own career to take off. She was jealous of the spotlight and the attention that Spencer was getting. So, one night, she did an interview with a tabloid. She was paid a lot of money, but the interview was pretty negative, and it ended their relationship. It also cost Spencer a few jobs. Luckily, her agent at the time was able to pull a few strings and keep the damage to a minimum."

"That's terrible."

"Yeah, it was pretty awful. It was a huge internal scandal, and Spencer didn't talk to anyone for months. It's really hard to find people you can trust in this industry. You have to be really careful who you let into your life."

"Wow," was all I could manage to say once again.

I tried not to, but the only thing I could think of was that

Jen had the exact same name as one of my exes. It was a small coincidence, but still.

"I never really thought about it that way. I guess there are a lot of things that I have never thought about when it comes to this."

"There are," Rebecca replied. "It can be hard, especially when you're on set. I know this isn't easy, but please don't take anything personally. Sometimes, I can get caught up in my own head. It's a hard habit to break."

"I think I can relate to that," I smiled.

"So, if you have any questions, or if you're not sure, or if you need someone to talk to, please don't hesitate to reach out, okay? My door is always open."

"Thanks," I nodded. "That means a lot."

"Of course," Rebecca smiled. "We're a team now."

Rebecca turned and made her way down the row of trailers, and I couldn't help but think that maybe this whole fake PR thing wasn't going to be the worst. Maybe we could make this work after all.

———

THE NEXT COUPLE of weeks were a whirlwind of activity. Between Spencer's press schedule, the final days of shooting, and the added intensity of our newfound relationship, we had very little time to spend alone, so when we did we made the most of it.

In fact, most of our alone time together consisted of quickie sessions in Spencer's trailer while we were on set, or stolen moments behind the set tents when no one was looking.

We were careful to make sure that we weren't seen being too affection together outside of set, and the secrecy was both exhilarating and exhausting.

The upside was that I had never been more sexually satisfied in my life. The downside was that we were always hiding. It was exhausting. But, also, the sneaking around was undeniably incredibly hot.

I'd never had an illicit affair before. Let alone with a beautiful movie star who always seemed to be flanked by a half dozen helpers. The secrecy only heightened the sexual tension between us. It was intense, and exciting, and intoxicating.

But, I was still trying to wrap my mind around the idea that my life was now a clandestine affair. This was all so foreign to me, and I was struggling to adjust to the changes.

I could tell that Spencer was, too.

But, despite the stress and the fear, we were making it work.

Our little bubble of bliss was holding steady.

Spencer was filming late, so we decided to meet at a local Italian restaurant for a late dinner. It was a quaint, little hole-in-the-wall place, and I was looking forward to enjoying a nice, quiet meal together.

When I arrived, I was shown to a table in the back corner, where I ordered a glass of red wine and waited for Spencer to arrive.

I was just about to order when Spencer bounced through the private back door. We'd learned all the sneaking around tricks.

"Hi, sorry I'm late," she whispered as she leaned in to hug me. "Rebecca was going over some things for tomorrow."

"It's okay," I smiled, leaning into her embrace. "I haven't ordered yet."

Spencer looked gorgeous, and I couldn't help but admire how effortlessly beautiful she was. She had changed out of her wardrobe from the shoot, and was wearing a pair of jeans and a simple white t-shirt. Her long, dark hair was pulled back into a low ponytail, and her makeup was fresh and natural.

"Good," she said. "Because I am starving."

Spencer reached across the table and grabbed my hand, squeezing it lightly. I could feel a blush creep up my neck and onto my cheeks.

"Me too," I replied, trying to ignore the heat radiating off my skin. "What are you in the mood for?"

"I think I'll get the spaghetti," she replied, not even bothering to look at the menu.

"Good choice," I nodded. "That's what I'm thinking, too."

Spencer gave me a warm smile. "Great minds think alike."

Just as I was about to ask the waiter for another glass of wine, a woman in her mid-thirties approached the table, nervously twiddling her pen and pad of paper.

"Ms. Wolf?" she asked, her voice barely audible.

Spencer smiled kindly. "Yes?"

"Hi, um, well, I'm a huge fan, and I was wondering if I could have your autograph?"

"Of course," Spencer replied graciously, taking the pen and paper the woman held out. "What's your name?"

"Jennifer."

Spencer wrote a quick note and handed the paper back to the woman, who stared down at it reverently.

"Thank you so much!" she gushed.

"You're very welcome," Spencer smiled. "Enjoy your meal."

The woman stood frozen, as if unsure what to do next. After a moment, she finally nodded and turned away.

I watched the woman retreat and couldn't help but notice how the rest of the patrons seemed to stare at our table, some even snapping surreptitious photos. It was the first time I had noticed it, and suddenly I was hyper aware of the people around us.

It was an odd sensation, being on display.

"Are you okay?" Spencer asked, reaching across the table and squeezing my hand.

I forced a smile and nodded. "Yeah, I'm fine."

"Are you sure?" she pressed, her brow furrowing. "You seem... off."

I sighed, shaking my head. "I'm sorry, it's nothing. It's just... everyone is staring."

Spencer glanced around the room, her eyes landing on the various tables who were clearly trying - and failing - to be discreet.

"Ignore them," she said, her voice barely above a whisper. "It's part of the role."

"I know," I sighed, shaking my head again. "I'm sorry, it's just... new."

Spencer gave me a small smile and nodded. "It is, and it's not. Look, the staring and the photos and the rumors, they're just part of the package. I'm not gonna lie, it sucks sometimes, but you get used to it."

"How?" I asked, trying to wrap my brain around the concept.

Spencer shrugged. "By reminding yourself that it's just a job. Yeah, the attention can be intense, but at the end of the day, it's all just part of the process. You have to remember that none of it is real."

"None of it is real?" I repeated, a feeling of dread starting to creep into the pit of my stomach.

"Well, I mean, not really," Spencer replied, seeming to choose her words carefully. "Like, yeah, the movies and the shows, they're real. And the acting and the work, that's all real, too. But, the rest of it, the fans and the attention, it's just a product. It's part of the show. The persona, the image, that's all just marketing."

"Oh."

My heart sank as some sort of sadness washed over me.

"Lauren," she said, her voice soft and her eyes pleading. "I didn't mean it like that. What we have, it's real. But, the public, that's just part of my job. The fame, the attention, the notoriety, that's just the nature of the beast. It's something I've learned to deal with."

"But, what does that mean for us?" I asked, the dread creeping up further in my chest.

"I don't know," she sighed, looking defeated. "Honestly, I think we're going to have to figure that out together. All I know is that I care about you, and I want to see where this goes. I want to keep seeing you. And, yeah, maybe it's stupid and naïve and selfish, but I don't care. I'm a big girl. I can make my own decisions. And I'm choosing you."

I couldn't help but smile, the warmth of her words spreading through my chest like wildfire.

"I'm choosing you too," I said, feeling a sense of relief wash over me. "But, what about the media and the fans? How do we deal with that?"

"Well," Spencer replied, leaning back in her chair. "The first thing we have to do is lay low. We shouldn't let many people know about us. At least not yet. The more secretive we are, the better."

I nodded, understanding. "Okay, but what about Chris? Aren't you guys going to have to be seen together for the press stuff?"

"Yes," she said, a mischievous smile spreading across her face. "But, that's different. That's just business. It's all just part of the deal."

"So, what, are we just gonna have to sneak around the whole time? Keep this a secret? I don't know how I feel about that," I admitted. "It seems like it'll be really hard to keep this going."

"Well, it won't be easy, but if we're careful, and we're smart, we ABSOLUTELY can make it work." Spencer too a deep breath and reached out her hand to take mine. "I wish I could take away all of your fears. All I can ask is that you trust me on this one."

"Yeah, but what about the rest of the crew and everyone on set? How are we gonna explain why we're always together?"

Spencer took a deep breath and let it out slowly. "That's the tough part. We're going to have to be extra careful. I'll talk to Rebecca and see if we can work something out."

"Work what out?" I asked, still feeling the nerves in my fingers.

"You know, a cover story, an excuse for us to be together all the time. Something that won't draw suspicion."

"Like what?"

Spencer thought for a moment before a smile spread across her lips.

"We'll tell them that I've hired you on as my full-time assistant. That way, no one will question why we're always together. It's the easy solution. Just for now."

"Okay," I nodded, my mind still reeling from the possibility of keeping our relationship a secret. "I guess I can do that."

"Good," Spencer said, her face breaking into a wide grin. "Now, let's get out of here. I've missed you."

We quickly paid for our food and snuck out the beck door onto an alleyway where Spencer's driver was waiting.

Without warning, Spencer reached out and pulled me into a dark corner for a passionate kiss. The feeling of Spencer's lips on mine were like a jolt of electricity. I felt her body melt into the actress, as if we were two pieces of a puzzle finally fitting together.

Spencer's mouth was hot and demanding, her tongue exploring mine eagerly. I could feel my body responding, my heart racing and my breath quickening. I lost myself in the kiss, the world around us fading away.

Finally, Spencer pulled back, her eyes dark with desire. "Damn, baby, I've been wanting to do that all day."

My cheeks flushed, and my body tingling with anticipation.

"Come on," Spencer said, taking my hand and leading me to the car. "Let's go back to my room. I have a few things I want to show you."

Ten painfully long minutes later, and we were back at the hotel.

When we got to Spencer's room, I followed my actress inside and closed the door behind us. Spencer immediately took my hand and led me to the bed, gently pushing me down onto the soft mattress. My heart raced as I looked up at Spencer, who was gazing down at me with lust-filled eyes.

"Now," Spencer said, her voice low and seductive. "Let's get you out of these clothes."

Spencer began slowly unbuttoning my shirt, her fingertips brushing against the sensitive skin of my chest. My breath caught in my throat as Spencer leaned in and began planting soft kisses along my collarbone. I let out a small moan as Spencer's hands moved lower, undoing my jeans and sliding them off my hips.

"Spencer," I breathed, my body aching with desire.

"Shhh," Spencer whispered, placing a finger to my lips. "Let me take care of you."

I nodded, my eyes fluttering closed as Spencer's hands continued their exploration of my body. My heart pounded in my chest as Spencer's fingers slid beneath the waistband of her panties, teasing my slick excitement.

"Oh God," I gasped, my hips bucking involuntarily.

Spencer smiled wickedly, her eyes locking with mine as her fingers slid inside my wetness. I moaned, my back arching as Spencer's skilled fingers stroked my sensitive bud.

My body trembled as waves of pleasure crashed over me, my climax building rapidly. I clung to Spencer, my nails digging into the actress's back.

"Spencer," I cried, my body writhing in ecstasy.

Spencer kissed me deeply, her tongue dancing with mine as her fingers increased their tempo. My body exploded with pleasure, my cries muffled by Spencer's insistent mouth.

Spencer's kisses became gentler, her fingers slowing their pace as I came down from my euphoric high. My breath was ragged, my heart pounding in my chest.

"Holy shit," I breathed, my body tingling with the aftershocks of my orgasm.

Spencer smiled down at me, a look of satisfaction on her face. "Mmm," she murmured, leaning in and kissing my neck. "You taste delicious."

I laughed, my body still trembling. "Wow," was all I could manage.

"Did you enjoy that?" Spencer asked, her voice low and seductive.

I nodded, unable to form words. All of my anxieties from the evening had dissolved into bliss.

"Good," Spencer said, a smile tugging at the corner of her lips. "Because there's plenty more where that came from."

My heart skipped a beat at the thought.

I was in for a wonderfully long night.

16

THE NEXT MORNING, Spencer and I woke early to the sound of her phone buzzing with notifications and back-to-back calls. Rolling over in the oversized bed, she reached for the blaring device.

"It's Rebecca," she groaned as she rubbed the sleep from her eyes.

"What does she want, this early in the morning?" I asked, suppressing a yawn of my own. We'd had a very long evening the night before.

"She's here. Downstairs. In the lobby." Spencer sat up in bed with a start.

"Rebecca is downstairs? Right now?" I couldn't hide the panic in my voice.

"Yes," Spencer sighed, running a hand through her hair. "She wants to come up and talk."

"To you or us? What does she want?"

"I'm not sure, but it can't be good." Spencer's brow furrowed, and I could see the worry written all over her face.

"Do you want me to stay while you talk to her? Or, should I leave? " I offered, trying to be helpful. Mostly though, I just wanted to be part of whatever conversation there was to be had. I liked being part of "Team Spencer."

"No, no," she insisted, shaking her head. "It's fine. Really. Just let me go downstairs and see what she wants."

I nodded and watched as Spencer threw on some clothes and headed for the door.

"Just stay put. I'll be back in a few." She gave me a quick peck on the cheek before disappearing through the door.

I waited impatiently in the hotel room, wondering what Rebecca could possibly want. Surely it was nothing, right? Maybe she was just coming to check in with Spencer. After all, she was her manager.

But, if that was the case, why couldn't they have talked over the phone? Why did she need to come all the way out to the hotel?

It didn't make any sense.

Something was up, and I had a sinking feeling in the pit of my stomach.

After what seemed like an eternity, Spencer returned with Rebecca in lock step beside her. Her expression was unreadable.

"So, what did she say?" I asked, the anxiety is my voice apparent.

Spencer sighed, shaking her head. "There's been a change in plans. Apparently, the studio execs want to try a new tactic. They think it'll be more effective guerrilla marketing if the main actors have a staged, on-set relationship."

I couldn't believe my ears. "Are you serious?"

"I'm afraid so," Spencer sighed, running a hand through her hair. "I tried to explain that was not an option, but apparently, they don't care."

"Who are they going to match you up with then?" My stomach churned at the thought.

"Chris," Spencer shrugged.

"Chris King? Your costar?"

"Yep," she said, shaking her head. "Apparently, they've already spoken to him, and he's on board."

"What the fuck?"

"I know," she groaned. "It's insane."

"Well, what are you going to do?"

"What can I do?" Spencer shrugged. "It's my job. It's what I signed up for. I have a media obligation clause in my contract, and the money men at the studio don't like being told no."

"So, you're going to pretend to date Chris? Your co-star?"

"Yes."

"For how long?"

"Until the movie is done. Probably a few months, tops."

I was silent. I couldn't believe what I was hearing.

"I know," she sighed, shaking her head. "It's nuts."

"That's putting it mildly."

"Look, I'm not happy about it either. But, I don't have a choice. This is the deal. It's part of the job."

I sat down on the bed, my mind racing. I couldn't believe this was happening. I couldn't believe that after all we had shared, everything we had experienced, that Spencer was now being forced to pretend to be in a relationship with someone else. It was a punch to the gut, and it hurt.

"I'm sorry, Lauren."

I looked up at her, and I could see the pain in her eyes. She was hurting, too. This wasn't what she wanted, either.

"I can't even imagine what you must be feeling right now."

I sighed, shaking my head. "Honestly, I don't even know. It's like I'm in a daze. This whole thing is just... surreal. It's not at all what I was expecting."

Her words were like a knife in my chest, piercing my

heart. I knew she was right, but I didn't want to admit it. I didn't want to face the reality of our situation.

"I know," I sighed. "I'm just trying to wrap my head around all of it. It's a lot to process."

"So, when does this fake relationship have to begin?" Spencer asked, slumping down onto the suite's couch.

"Well, now that we're working with Chris' team and his schedule too, we are going to have to be flexible. He's booked on a media blitz in New York this weekend, so they want you to fly up and have a very public dinner and night out with him. Paparazzi from door to door, some quick shots of you all at the restaurant. You'd be able to be back by Monday."

"I have to go to New York City, with Chris?" Spencer looked appalled.

"Just for one day, yes. Then you'll both come back here and shoot the last few scenes together. On-set leaked pictures and all that. This is the best plan the studio can offer. They want a real-looking relationship. They think the chemistry between the two of you will help promote the movie and drive ticket sales."

"What's wrong with some standard, fake PR stint? An on-set feud or maybe Chris can fake it with one of the producers. It's worked for plenty of actors and actresses before," Spencer grumbled.

"This isn't negotiable," Rebecca stated. "If you want to stay playing nice with the studio, you need to do what they say."

"I know, I know. I just... This is crazy."

"It's not the craziest thing I've heard, trust me. And, it's only for a little while. Then, you can have your normal life back. No more pretending."

Spencer nodded. Rebecca stood up and collected her purse.

"Now, I'll leave you to get packed while I arrange your travel. Just try to relax until then!" Rebecca sighed, walking towards the door. "We'll all get through this. It is just a few weeks. Remember to smile for the cameras and think about the box-office!"

With that, Rebecca was gone just as fast as she had arrived.

"So, what are you thinking?" Spencer asked, her tone somber as we were finally alone again.

"I don't know," I replied, shaking my head. "This is all so fucked up."

"Tell me about it."

"What are you going to do?"

Spencer shrugged. "I don't know. I guess I'll just have to do what they ask. It's not like I have a choice."

"Is there anything I can do?"

"No," Spencer said, shaking her head. "Unfortunately, this is something I have to deal with on my own. You're still new to this. It would only complicate things."

"But, I want to help," I protested, not willing to give up so easily.

"I know," Spencer smiled, taking her hand. "And, I appreciate it. But, the best way for you to help right now is just to be here, by my side."

"I can do that."

"Good," Spencer nodded. "Because I'm going to need all the support I can get. We're going to need to support each other so this doesn't have to be a bumpy ride."

Standing, she walked over to the edge of the bed where I was still sitting. She took my hand from my lap and interwove our fingers. Her touch sent electricity down both arms, and I felt like I could take a deep breath for the first time since Rebecca had walked through the door.

"How about we have a date when I get back? A real one.

Dinner and a night out and no one but us. Please. I wanna make up the fact that I have to spend the weekend away."

"That sounds amazing," I replied.

"Good," Spencer murmured, her face softening into a smile. "Now, I've got to pack. Do you wanna stay and keep me company? We can order in some room service and take a grounding bath after I finish."

The offer was tempting, but I needed a moment to process the last few days. I needed a moment to myself.

"I think I should probably head home," I sighed. "I'm tired, and I haven't been home in a while. I should probably check in and tend to all the things I've been putting off the last week."

Spencer nodded, though I could see some sadness in her eyes. "Okay, I understand. I am sorry, again, Lauren. I know this is a weird situation. I hope it's not scared you away."

"Not at all," I whispered, trying to convince both of us that it was the truth. "I just need some rest. It's been a long week."

"Okay, okay," she sighed dramatically and adorably. "Text me though. It's going to be a hellish weekend as is, and I'll be missing you."

She pulled me to my feet and kissed me quickly, and we walked together to the door.

"I'll call you later," I promised, as she kissed me one last time.

Her fingers wrapped around the base of my neck and held me close with a gentle strength. Her lips were firm against mine as she said goodbye with her tongue.

Part of me hated leaving her, but I knew I needed a few days to process everything that had happened in such a whirlwind week. Stepping out into the hallway, I shot her one last smile. "I'll see you on Monday. Just a couple of days."

"Just a couple of days," she agreed with a soft grin. "See you soon, Lauren."

"See you soon, Spencer."

Closing the door after myself, I leaned against it and heaved a sigh. It was as though she'd kept all the oxygen in the room with her.

The hallway felt cold and lonely without her, and I knew that if I didn't leave now, I would knock on her door and fall right back into her bed.

This was going to be a long few days.

17

I DROVE around for an hour before I finally headed back to my apartment. I'd needed some time to clear my head, and blasting music with the windows down as I cruised back roads through town gave me just the fresh air I needed to think.

It was early evening when I arrived, and as soon as I stepped through the door, I was greeted by Julie and Allie, who were sprawled on the couch watching TV.

"Well, hello there!" Julie exclaimed, her eyes wide as I walked in. "Where have you been?"

"I was just out," I shrugged, trying to play it cool.

"Out? Out where?" Allie pressed, leaning forward.

"Just out," I repeated, shaking my head. "I just went for a drive."

"A drive? For two days?" Julie asked, her eyebrows raised skeptically. She turned towards Allie and fake whispered, "Lauren didn't come home last night. I think she was out on a date with someone."

"A date?!" Julie exclaimed. "It wouldn't have been with a particularly sexy actress, now would it?"

I wasn't in the mood to gossip. And, quite frankly, I

wasn't ready to talk to either of my friends about Spencer just yet. At that moment, all I really wanted was to crawl into bed and rest.

"I was just working," I half fibbed. It was true that we had talked work, so it didn't full like a full-out lie.

"WORKING? What could you be doing with Spencer Wolf that would keep you out all night?" Allie asked, wiggling her eyebrows.

"Oh, come on," I groaned, rolling my eyes. "You guys know it's not like that."

"Not like what?" Julie teased. "Not like you're sleeping with a movie star?"

"No!" I exclaimed, my cheeks flushing red.

"Come on," Allie giggled. "You have to give us something! What's she like? Is she a good kisser?"

"No comment!" I shot back, my blush deepening. I turned and headed for my bedroom, eager to escape my friends' probing questions.

But, I knew I couldn't avoid them forever. I would have to tell them the truth eventually. They were my best friends, after all.

However, for now, I just wanted to enjoy the memory of my time with Spencer, before reality came crashing down on me again.

I flopped down onto my bed, my mind racing.

This was really happening. I was really dating a famous actress. I was really dating Spencer Wolf.

It seemed surreal. It felt like a dream.

I pinched myself to make sure I was awake.

Ouch.

Yep. Definitely awake.

I couldn't help but smile as I thought about the night before.

We'd spent the night exploring each other's bodies, learning what made the other tick, and it was magical. There had never been anyone like her before.

As I lay there in bed, I couldn't help but think about what our future might hold.

Would we be able to make our relationship work?

Or would the pressures of her job, and the spotlight that came with it, be too much for us to handle?

Only time would tell.

But, in that moment, I was hopeful.

Hopeful that we could make it work.

Hopeful that we could have a future together.

Hopeful that she was the one.

I fell asleep with visions of Spencer dancing through my mind.

18

THE NEXT MORNING, I woke up feeling refreshed and ready to tackle the day. I'd needed the sleep, and I felt much better after a good night's rest.

As I walked into the kitchen, I was greeted by Allie and Julie, who were sipping coffee and eating breakfast.

"Morning," I mumbled, rubbing the sleep from my eyes.

"Morning," Julie replied, smiling at me. "How did you sleep?"

"Like a rock," I sighed. "I was exhausted."

"Well, you must have had a long night," Allie teased, grinning at me.

"Oh, stop," I groaned, rolling my eyes. "You guys are impossible."

"So, are you going to tell us what happened?" Julie pressed, her eyes wide with curiosity.

"Nothing happened," I replied, shaking my head. "We just talked."

"Talked? For two days?"

"Well, we also slept," I clarified.

"Together?"

"Yes, together," I sighed, exasperated.

"So, nothing else happened?"

I hesitated. I knew if I told them the truth, they would never let it go.

"No," I said finally, shaking my head.

"Damn," Julie muttered, looking disappointed.

"I have to say, I'm a little surprised," Allie added. "I thought for sure there would be more juicy details."

"Well, there aren't," I replied, my tone short.

I couldn't help but feel a little annoyed at my friends for pressuring me into talking about my relationship with Spencer. I knew they meant well, but I wasn't ready to share all the intimate details just yet. It was still too new, and too special, to me.

"Okay, okay," Julie sighed, holding up her hands in mock surrender. "We'll stop asking questions. But, just know that when you're ready to talk, we're here for you."

"Thanks," I murmured, my tone softening. "I appreciate it."

I poured myself a cup of coffee and sat down at the table with my friends. I knew they were just looking out for me, but it was still a bit much for me to handle so early in the morning. I wanted to enjoy my time with Spencer before I had to deal with all of the pressures and expectations that came with dating a celebrity.

I sipped my coffee and listened as Julie and Allie talked about their plans for the day. It was nice to hear about normal, everyday things. It helped to ground me and reminded me that there was still a life beyond the spotlight.

Just then, my phone buzzed with an incoming text from Spencer.

'Can't wait to see you again. I miss you already.'

I couldn't help but smile as I read her words. She had such a way of making me feel special. It was a feeling I could get used to.

'Miss you, too,' I texted back. 'Monday can't come soon enough. Did you make it to NYC?'

'Yep, just got here. It's freezing!'

I laughed. 'It's supposed to snow later. I checked the weather.'

'Great. Just what I need. I miss your voice. Can I call?'

I hadn't even finished typing my reply when the phone rang on its own. Standing up, I stepped into my bedroom for privacy.

"Sorry," her voice broke through the static of the phone as I answered. "I couldn't wait. I just got back to my room and I was missing you desperately."

I imagined Spencer shivering in the cold New York weather. I wished I could be there with her, keeping her warm.

"Stay inside where it's warm. You have a fancy hotel room?"

"I do, but I'm already missing you in it."

"I'm missing you, too. What are you up to tonight?"

"I'm meeting some of the cast and the producers at a restaurant for dinner and drinks. Chris is supposed to pick me up so that we can be seen 'arriving together' as I'm sure the headlines tomorrow will phrase it."

"That sounds like fun."

"No," she said firmly, "it sounds like work. It's part of the deal. This movie is a big deal for both of us, and I have to play the game, as Rebecca likes to remind me. But the good news is that the filming should be over by the end of the month, and then we can really enjoy our time together. So, I'll call you when I get back to the hotel, and you can tell me all about your evening with the girls. Maybe you can have a glass of wine for me, and we can talk dirty."

I grinned as I thought about just how bad I'd be at dirty

talk over the phone. "I don't think I'd be very convincingly sexy on a call."

I could hear a smile in her voice as she hummed over the phone. "Well, practice does make perfect. We'll have to put some hours in to get you good."

"That sounds like hard work to me," I teased.

"Oh, baby, it is," she purred. "Now, go and enjoy your friends. I'll speak to you later. Be safe."

"You, too."

"Bye, baby." She hung up, and I switched off my cell, grinning. She makes me feel like a schoolgirl again. I couldn't wipe the silly grin off my face.

"Who was that?" Julie asked as I walked back into the kitchen.

"Just Spencer," I replied casually.

"You seem pretty happy to hear from her," Allie observed with a smirk.

"She's fun to talk to," I shrugged, trying to play it cool.

"Fun, huh? That's all?" Allie pressed, clearly not satisfied with my answer.

I sighed. "Look, I like her, okay? She's sweet and funny and charming. And, yes, I'll admit, it's exciting to hang around with someone who's famous. But, I'm also realistic. I don't know what any of us means for me yet. I mean, what if I'm just a fun time to have on set?"

"You don't know that," Julie interjected, her tone surprisingly defensive.

"Come on," I groaned, rolling my eyes. "I'm not an idiot. I know the score. She's a rich, successful movie star. I'm just some girl she met on a film set. I'm not delusional."

"You're not just some girl," Julie said, shaking her head. "You're an awesome, bad-ass bitch who deserves to be treated right. And, if Spencer can't see that, then she's an idiot."

"She's not an idiot," I sighed. "She's just...busy. And, caught up in PR stuff for this movie. I mean, she is Spencer Wolf, after all."

"I know," Julie said, her tone sympathetic. "But, that doesn't mean she has to treat you like an afterthought."

"She's not," I insisted. "It's just...it's complicated. This is all new for me. I've never dated anyone like her before."

"I know," Allie said, smiling. "But, you can handle it. You're Lauren, after all."

I smiled at her words. "Thanks, guys. I don't know what I'd do without you."

"Real question, though: have you ever actually seen any of her other, older movies?" Julie asked.

I thought for a long moment, racking my brain. I had to have seen something Spencer had done in her earlier career, right? And yet, I couldn't think of a single one other than her latest blockbuster.

"I guess I haven't seen any of them," I confessed sheepishly.

"Well that is totally unacceptable!" Julie faked outrage. "I think that answers the question of what we have planned for the rest of the day. We should have a Spencer Wolf movie marathon!"

"I second that!" Allie agreed, clapping her hands together excitedly.

I rolled my eyes. "Oh, come on. You guys can't be serious."

"Oh, we're serious," Julie said, nodding her head. "It's time to educate you on all things Spencer Wolf."

"Fine," I sighed, throwing my hands up in defeat. "Let's do this. But, if we're going to sit through a whole day of movies...I think we're going to need some snacks."

"Absolutely second to that," Allie laughed.

AN HOUR and one snack run later, and it was time for 6 back to back hours of Spencer's film portfolio.

The three of us settled onto the couch, ready to start the marathon. We began with Spencer's first film, which was a coming-of-age story about a young girl trying to find her place in the world. It was beautifully shot and acted, and I found herself captivated by Spencer's performance.

This was the sort of project she was talking about. The sort of work she used to do before she got cornered into the "hot, action star" role. I could tell there was a passion in this work that she didn't seem to have, even on our current set.

"She's amazing," Julie commented, her eyes glued to the screen.

"She really is," I agreed, a smile tugging at the corners of my lips.

"I can't believe you're so close with her," Allie exclaimed, shaking her head in disbelief.

"Me neither," I laughed. "It's all so surreal, especially seeing her on screen like this."

"How is it going, by the way?" Julie asked, finally tearing her gaze away from the TV to look at me.

"It's... good," I said, nodding slowly. "Really good, actually."

"I'm happy for you," Allie smiled, patting my arm. "You deserve to be with someone who makes you happy...no matter what sort of relationship you all are delusional trying to pretend is casual."

I couldn't help but smile at her words. "Thanks, guys. I appreciate that."

I felt a warm feeling wash over me. It was nice to know that my friends were supportive of my relationship with Spencer, even if it was a bit unconventional.

"So, ready for movie number 2? It's a jump to full action and sweaty muscle shots. Buckle up. It gets sexy," Julie laughed.

"I'm ready," I said, sitting back and settling in for the next film.

The movie started, and we were immediately plunged into an action-packed world of adventure and intrigue. I found myself on the edge of my seat as Spencer's character raced against time to save the day.

I watched in awe as she leapt from building to building, scaled walls, and took down bad guys with ease. It was a completely different side of her that I hadn't seen before, but I was captivated.

After the movie, the three of us sat in silence, taking in everything we'd just seen. It was clear that we were all blown away by Spencer's performance.

"Okay, I'll admit it," I said finally. "She was pretty good in this movie, too."

"Pretty good?" Julie scoffed. "She was amazing! I don't think I've ever seen anyone move the way she did in that movie. Lordy, that was hot."

"I know," I agreed. "It was like she was born to play that role."

We all sat in silence for a moment, thinking about the amazing performance we'd just witnessed. It was clear that Spencer Wolf was a very talented actress.

"So," Allie said finally, turning to me. "What's the next movie on your list?"

"Well, there's the action one, the rom com, the spy thriller, the Oscar-winning drama, the Oscar-nominated drama, and then the one where she gets naked a lot and makes out with a bunch of other women," I said, checking the list of Spencer's movies that Julie had helped me make earlier that day.

"Ooh, ooh," Julie said excitedly. "I vote for the one where she gets naked a lot!"

"Me, too," Allie agreed, nodding her head. "I want to see how far she's willing to go for her art."

The three of us laughed. I couldn't help but feel excited to see the rest of Spencer's movies. I loved watching her on screen, and I wanted to learn more about the actress I was dating.

The next few hours were a blur of action, romance, and drama as we binge watched the rest of Spencer's films.

There was one movie that really stood out to me. It was a quiet, independent film that told the story of two people from different worlds falling in love. The chemistry between the lead actress, which was Spencer, and the leading man, was palpable.

It was the sort of role that Spencer seemed to be made for, and her performance was electric. She brought a depth and a complexity to her character that was captivating to watch. It was easy to see why she had won so many awards for the role.

As the credits rolled, Allie and Julie were both in tears. We all sat in silence for a few moments, taking in the beauty and emotion of the film.

"That was amazing," Allie finally said, wiping away a tear.

"I know," Julie agreed, shaking her head in disbelief. "I can't believe how talented Spencer is. She's an amazing actress."

I nodded in agreement, still speechless after watching the movie. I had never seen anything like it. It was emotional and raw, and it left me feeling moved in a way I had never experienced before.

I stood up and stretched. "Well, I don't know about you guys, but I'm starving. How about some pizza?"

"Yes, please!" Allie exclaimed, her eyes lighting up.

"Me, too!" Julie chimed in. "And, I think we've earned it after watching all those movies.

The three of us ordered a pizza and settled in to watch more movies. We talked and laughed as we devoured slice after slice of cheesy goodness. It was a perfect afternoon, and it was exactly what I needed. I felt relaxed and happy as I spent time with my two best friends.

19

A FEW ROUNDS of drinks later, and, just as we were about to press play on another Spencer-centric movie, Julie's phone started buzzing to life.

"Damn, girl," I commented. "Who is blowing you up like that?"

"I don't know," Julie replied, crossing the room to fetch her device. "But that's not my text tone. It's my news app alert tone. Weird."

"What's the breaking news?" Allie asked eagerly.

Julie looked at her phone in silence for a few moments. Her finger scrolled through seemingly story after story. And the entire time, not a word.

Something was up.

Allie must have felt it too, because she stood and crossed the room towards Julie. "What is it, Jules? Let me see."

Julie tipped the phone Allie's way, and the two women huddled together reading the headlines.

"Oh," Allie gulped.

"What is it?" I asked. This was getting weird. "Come on, guys. What are you looking at?"

"It's Spencer...It looks like she and Chris King are on a

date or something in NYC. There are pics of them leaving a hotel, going out to dinner with his arms all around her, and then back to the hotel."

Both of my friends looked up at me expectantly. They had no idea that I knew it was just PR, and I wasn't sure I was in a position to tell them just yet. So instead, I just shrugged half heartedly.

"Yeah, they're in New York doing some press tour stops. I think the whole production team went out for dinner and drinks afterwards," I muttered.

"These look like a lot more than just a production dinner," Julie huffed under her breath. "His paws are all over her. Look."

She reached out her hand and stuck the images in my face.

I took the phone from her and was immediately met with a whole slideshow of pictures of blurry paparazzi pictures of Spencer and Chris making their way out of the back door of a restaurant. The headlines couldn't have been more sensational.

"Spencer Wolf and Chris King: On Set Affair? Hot Hollywood Lovebirds Look Close After Romantic Dinner in NYC"

"Spencer and Chris: An ITEM? Hollywood's Hot Duo Caught Canoodling After Wild Night Out on the Town"

"Spencer and Chris: The Second Coming of Brangelina? Hollywood's Power Players Seen Together After Hours!"

I had to admit, it looked bad. I felt a pang of jealousy in my stomach as I scrolled through the photos. Seeing the woman I had spent the better part of the last 6 weeks wrapped up in bed with now in someone else's arms made my insides churn. I felt my mouth go dry as I scrolled through the images.

"Uhh, did you know about this?" Julie asked, leaping onto the couch beside me for a better look at the phone.

"Yeah," I replied, trying my hardest to keep my voice steady. I didn't want my friends to know that I knew all bout the plan for the night and went along with it without complaint. That seemed suddenly embarrassing now.

They were both staring intently while we examined these scandalous shots on our phones.

"I'm sure it's not what it looks like," Allie whispered.

"I don't see what else it could be," Julie scoffed.

"They had a cast party with the director and producers tonight," I replied, ignoring my friend's snark. "They called in the paps themselves. It's a marketing thing for the movie."

"Is that really how it works?" Allie asked.

"I guess so," I shrugged. Just as I was scrolling through the 5th article in a row, my phone lit up with Spencer's name. Wanting to talk to her more than anything, I quietly stood up with my best fake yawn. "I think I'm going to call it a night."

"I think someone just got a damage control booty call," Julie laughed.

"And I think you had one too many margs," I sighed. "Seriously though, I'm going to bed and no one has to worry."

With that, I made my way back to my bedroom before Spencer's call went to voicemail.

"Hey," was about all I could muster as I answered the line.

"Hey, babe," her voiced cooed from a thousand miles away. "I hope I'm not pulling you away from your friends."

"No," I chuckled. "You had perfect timing, actually. Julie's phone went crazy when the pictures of you and Chris dropped."

"Oh, shit," she sighed. "Have those already gone up? I swear, they get faster at uploading by the day."

"Oh, yeah. They are definitely out there." I crawled into

bed and tried not to worry about the distance between us in this moment.

There was a moment of silence on the other line as I heard Spencer shuffle around on her end.

"Wow," she finally replied. "They really got their money's worth with these pictures. Chris got a little handsy for sure. God, Lauren, I'm so sorry you had to be bombarded with that."

"Yeah. Yeah." It was all I could stay. "I mean, I knew it was coming. That doesn't make it not feel super shitty to see my girlfriend's name plastered all over social media with some chiseled hunk of a dude."

"Girlfriend, huh?"

There was a moment of silence as I realize what I'd just declared. We'd thrown around a few words, but this was something different, and I couldn't tell if I had overstepped or not.

"Well, I'm not sure what other word to use," I admitted. "What do you think?"

"I think I absolutely adore the term 'girlfriend' for us." I could hear the smile in her voice and wondered if she could hear my own content smile over the phone.

"Just a couple of girlfriends who have to pretend one of them is in a relationship with a sexy Hollywood boyfriend," I sighed. The words came out more frustrated than I was expecting.

"Babyyyy," Spencer moaned sadly. "Oh, you're mad at me, aren't you?"

"No, no. I'm not. I'm just...something. I don't know. I'm probably just tired and a little drunk."

It was true. I really wasn't mad at Spencer. No matter how much I felt uncomfortable about the situation, I just couldn't muster being angry. Just...sad.

"Can I make it up to you? Maybe the mood isn't right for

the sexy night I had in mind, but what if I read to you? It's about time I returned the favor."

My heart quickly skipped a beat as I curled under the covers and drifted off to Spencer picking up where we left off in my favorite book. Her voice so soft and tender. Her interest in my passions obvious.

This was the Spencer I was falling for.

And just as I realized how much I *was* falling, I drifted off into sleep to the beautiful notes of Spencer's voice.

20

THE REST of the weekend flew by, and before I knew it, it was Monday morning. I woke up bright and early, eager to get to work and see Spencer again. I couldn't wait to see her after being apart for the weekend.

I arrived at the hotel and went up to Spencer's suite. When I walked into the room, she greeted me with a smile.

"Hey, you," she said, her eyes sparkling.

"Hi," I replied, grinning like an idiot.

We stood there, gazing at each other for a few moments.

"I've missed you," she said finally, her voice low and husky.

"I've missed you, too," I breathed, my heart racing.

She took a step closer, closing the distance between us. She cupped my cheek in her palm and looked into my eyes.

"I've been thinking about you all weekend," she murmured, her thumb gently caressing my skin.

"Really?"

"Oh, yes," she whispered. "And now you're finally here."

She leaned down and pressed her lips against mine, her kiss soft and sweet. My heart fluttered, and I felt like I was floating.

Her arm slipped around my waist, and she pulled me closer. Our bodies pressed together, and I felt the warmth of her skin through her clothes.

I wrapped my arms around her neck, savoring the feeling of her body against mine. Her tongue darted out and licked my lower lip, and I opened my mouth to let her in.

My head was spinning as her tongue explored my mouth. She tasted like mint and something else that was completely her. It was intoxicating.

Her hand slid up my back, sending shivers down my spine. She tangled her fingers in my hair and gently tugged, tilting my head back. I moaned as she trailed kisses along my jaw and down my neck.

My heart was pounding in my chest. I could feel my pulse racing as her lips made their way back up to my ear. She nibbled on my earlobe before whispering in my ear, "I want you, Lauren."

I felt a jolt of desire between my legs. "I want you, too," I breathed, my voice trembling slightly.

She pulled away and looked into my eyes. "Are you sure?"

"Yes," I replied, my voice barely above a whisper.

She took my hand and led me over to the bed. She sat down and pulled me onto her lap so that I was straddling her. She kissed me again, her lips soft and warm against mine.

Her hands moved up my thighs and under my skirt, her fingers brushing against my panties. I moaned as she began to stroke me through the thin fabric.

"You're so wet," she murmured, her breath hot against my skin.

I could only whimper in response as she slipped her fingers under my panties and touched me. She circled my clit, sending shockwaves of pleasure through my body. I gasped as she plunged two fingers inside me, her thumb still rubbing my clit. I clutched at her shoulders, my nails digging into her skin.

I closed my eyes and leaned my head back as she continued to stroke me, bringing me closer and closer to the edge.

The pressure was building inside me, and I could feel myself teetering on the brink of orgasm. I looked into Spencer's eyes, and she smiled at me, her expression full of desire.

"Come for me, Lauren," she whispered, her voice husky.

And I did. I came hard, my body trembling as the waves of pleasure crashed over me. I cried out, burying my face in her neck as I rode out the last aftershocks of my orgasm.

As my breathing returned to normal, I lifted my head to look at Spencer. She smiled at me, her eyes sparkling.

"That was amazing," I breathed.

"It was," she agreed, brushing a strand of hair from my face.

We sat there for a moment, gazing at each other. Then, she kissed me again, her lips soft and sweet. I lost myself in her kiss, my body aching for more.

She gently pulled away, smiling at me.

"I guess we should get ready for our date night," she said, her voice low. "I did plan a whole evening for us that goes way beyond these hotel walls."

"That sounds exciting," I murmured, still a little breathless. "That was also the absolute best start to a date I've ever experienced."

"Good," she said, leaning in to kiss me once more.

I melted against her, savoring the feeling of her lips on mine. She broke the kiss and stood, pulling me to my feet.

"Now, let me get you something to wear," she said, walking over to the closet and opening it up.

She pulled out a beautiful red dress and handed it to me.

"This is gorgeous," I breathed, running my fingers over the silky fabric.

"I think it will look lovely on you," she replied, smiling.

"Thank you," I said, taking the dress from her.

"You're welcome. Now, go and get changed," she instructed, gently pushing me towards the bathroom.

I did as I was told, and quickly slipped into the dress. It fit perfectly, accentuating my curves and making me feel sexy. I admired myself in the mirror, turning this way and that, admiring how good I looked.

I emerged from the bathroom to find Spencer dressed in a black suit with a white shirt. She looked stunning, and I couldn't help but stare at her.

"Wow, you look amazing," I said, my voice barely above a whisper.

"So do you," she replied, her voice husky. "That dress looks incredible on you."

She took my hand and led me to the door. We left the hotel room, and headed downstairs to the lobby. As we walked, I noticed that everyone seemed to be watching us. It was a strange sensation, but I tried to ignore it.

When we arrived at the lobby, I saw that a limo was waiting for us. The driver opened the door for us, and we climbed inside.

As soon as the door closed, I felt Spencer's arm slip around my waist, and she pulled me close.

"Hi," she murmured, her lips inches from mine.

"Hi," I breathed, my heart racing.

She leaned in and kissed me, her lips soft and warm against mine. My head spun as her tongue slipped into my mouth. I tangled my fingers in her hair, pulling her closer. I felt like I couldn't get enough of her.

The driver coughed discreetly from behind the partition

blocking the front seat, and we pulled apart, both breathless. We grinned at each other as the limo pulled up to the
restaurant.

The driver got out and opened the door for us, and we
stepped out into the cool night air. There were a few
paparazzi hanging around outside the restaurant, but they
seemed more interested in the celebrities arriving than the
two of us.

Spencer took my hand and led me inside. The hostess
greeted us and showed us to our table. It was tucked away in
a private corner of the restaurant, which I was grateful for. I
didn't want to share our evening with anyone else.

We sat down and perused the menu. After a few
minutes, the waiter came to take our order.

"What would you like, Lauren?" Spencer asked.

"I'll have the steak," I replied. "And a glass of red wine,
please."

"I think we'll both have the same," Spencer said, smiling
at me.

The waiter nodded and left us alone.

"This place is nice," I commented, looking around at the
elegant décor.

"It is," Spencer agreed. "I've been here a few times, and
the food is always good."

We chatted as we waited for our food. When it arrived,
we dug into it hungrily. The steak was delicious, and the
wine was perfectly paired with it.

We talked and laughed as we ate, enjoying each other's
company. It felt like we had known each other for years, not
just a few short weeks.

After we finished our meal, Spencer ordered us another
round of drinks. We sat and sipped our wine, our eyes
locked on each other.

The restaurant had emptied out except for the waitstaff

who had been instructed to give us privacy, and there was a quiet lull in the music.

"Would you like to dance?" Spencer asked, her voice low and husky.

"Yes," I breathed, my heart pounding in my chest.

She stood and held out her hand. I took it, and she led me to the dance floor. We began to sway to the music, our bodies pressed close together.

I looked up at her and smiled. "I've never danced with a woman before."

"I find that hard to believe," she murmured, her eyes dark with desire.

"It's true," I insisted. "You're the first."

She grinned, her eyes sparkling with amusement.

"Well, I'm honored," she said.

We continued to dance, our bodies moving together in perfect harmony. She held me close, her hands resting on the small of my back. I could feel the heat from her body through my dress, and I couldn't help but press myself closer to her.

I rested my head on her shoulder, breathing in her scent. She smelled like lavender and something else, something uniquely her. It was intoxicating.

I felt a tingle of desire low in my belly as we danced. I had never felt this way about anyone before, and it both excited and frightened me. I knew that Spencer was dangerous, but I couldn't seem to help myself.

The song came to an end, and I lifted my head to look at her. She smiled down at me, her eyes full of emotion.

"Lauren," she said softly, her voice husky. "You're so beautiful."

I blushed and looked away. Her hand cupped my chin, gently turning my face back towards her.

"Don't look away," she murmured. "I want to see your beautiful eyes."

I met her gaze, my heart pounding in my chest.

"You make me feel things I've never felt before," I whispered, my voice trembling slightly.

"I know," she breathed, her fingers stroking my cheek. "I feel it, too."

She leaned down and kissed me, her lips soft and warm against mine. My heart fluttered as I tasted her. She pulled me closer, her hands sliding down my back. I felt like I was melting into her. I'd never felt this way before.

We stood there, wrapped in each other's arms, our bodies pressed together. I never wanted the moment to end.

Spencer must have been reading my mind, because she leaned in and whispered in my ear, "Are you ready for Part 2 of the evening?"

"Part 2?" I asked with a smile. This was already the most amazing date I'd ever been on, and I couldn't imagine how Spencer could make it even better. "What does Part 2 entail?"

"Oh, it's a surprise," Spencer teased. "But, it will require a clothing change before we head that way."

"A clothing change?" I queried.

"Yes," Spencer chuckled. "I have another outfit for you."

"I think I could do that," I said with a grin. "Just lead the way."

Spencer led me off the dance floor and through a side door. We walked down a long, dimly lit hallway back towards the limo before speeding in the direction of Spencer's suite for our wardrobe swap. It was amazing how much she'd planned this all out.

Inside, there was a rack of clothes and a full-length mirror now set up in the sitting area.

When had she had the time to pull this off?

Spencer closed the door behind us and turned to me.

"Okay," she breathed, her voice low and husky. "Let's see what we can find for you to wear."

She began to rummage through the rack of clothes, looking for something that would suit me. I stood and watched her, my heart racing. The tension in the air was palpable.

After a moment, Spencer turned to me, holding up a skimpy black dress.

"What do you think of this one?" she asked, a wicked gleam in her eye.

"Um, it's...um..." I stuttered, my mouth suddenly dry.

Spencer laughed softly.

"Come on," she said, taking my hand. "Let's see how it looks on you."

She led me over to the full-length mirror and held the dress up against my body.

I looked at myself in the mirror and was surprised to see that I looked good. I felt a tingle of desire low in my belly as I imagined wearing the dress with Spencer by my side.

"I think it will look perfect on you," she breathed, her voice low and husky.

I shivered, feeling goosebumps break out on my arms.

"Okay," I said, my voice barely above a whisper.

"Here," she murmured, handing me the dress. "You can try it on."

I took the dress from her and began to unbutton my shirt. My hands were trembling slightly as I fumbled with the buttons. I could feel Spencer watching me, and I felt my cheeks flush.

As I took off my clothes, I saw Spencer's eyes wander over my body. I felt a jolt of desire low in my belly as she gazed at me.

When I was completely naked, I stood before her, my heart pounding.

She took a step towards me, her eyes dark with desire.

"You are so beautiful, Lauren," she breathed, her voice husky with emotion.

I felt a surge of confidence at her words. I stepped closer to her, closing the distance between us. I could feel the heat of her body, even through her clothes. She looked down at me, her eyes searching mine. I smiled up at her and leaned in, my lips brushing against hers. I felt her take a sharp breath in as I kissed her. Her arms snaked around my waist, pulling me close. I felt a jolt of electricity as our bodies pressed together. It was intoxicating. I ran my hands up her back, my fingers tangling in her hair. She deepened the kiss, her tongue probing my mouth. I moaned softly as her hands slid down to cup my ass.

I kissed her again, hungrily. She responded, her hands roaming my body, exploring every inch of me. She cupped my breast, her thumb brushing over my nipple, sending a jolt of pleasure through my body. I moaned softly, pressing myself against her, needing to feel more of her.

She gently pushed me back until I felt the wall against my back. She pinned me against it, her body pressed against mine. I could feel her arousal, and it made me ache for her.

She kissed me deeply, her tongue probing my mouth. I felt dizzy with desire.

Her hand slid between my legs, her fingers gently stroking me. I moaned as she touched me, my body trembling with need.

She trailed kisses down my neck, her tongue teasing my skin. I gasped as she nipped my collarbone, my hands fisting in her hair.

She continued to stroke me, her fingers sliding easily over my wetness. I moaned, my hips bucking against her hand.

She slipped two fingers inside me, curling them up to hit

that spot that drove me wild. I cried out, my head falling back against the wall. She pressed her body against mine, pinning me to the wall as she thrust her fingers into me, her thumb circling my clit with every stroke.

I was teetering on the edge, my body trembling as I clung to her. I looked down at her and our eyes locked. Her gaze was intense, full of desire and need. It was too much. I closed my eyes, unable to look at her anymore.

"Look at me, Lauren," she murmured.

I opened my eyes, looking down at her again. She smiled up at me, her eyes dark with desire.

"Come for me, Lauren," she whispered, her voice husky.

I came undone. My body shuddered as waves of pleasure crashed over me. I cried out, my nails digging into her shoulders as I rode out the last aftershocks of my orgasm.

I collapsed against her, my legs shaking.

Twice.

In one day.

On one amazing date.

How was this real?

She wrapped her arms around me, holding me close. I breathed in the scent of her, feeling safe and secure in her embrace.

She kissed my forehead, and we sat in silence for a few moments. I was content to be held by her, but a niggling thought kept poking at my brain.

I lifted my head to look at her, and she smiled down at me.

"What is it, babe?"

"I just can't believe how amazing this night has been," I whispered.

"And we still have a whole Part 2 ahead," she smiled. "Come on, let's pick you out an actual outfit. That last one was mostly just for my own benefit."

"So you tricked me with the sexy dress!" I teased, kissing at her laugh-crinkled cheek.

"I did not trick, I just wanted a little fashion show," Spencer winked back.

"There should be a much more suitable pair of jeans and a t-shirt stacked next to the dresses. I just couldn't resist seeing you in...and out...of one of those."

"I see," I said, giving her a peck on the lips.

As I pulled away, her hand darted out and grabbed my wrist.

"You're not getting off that easy," she murmured, her eyes sparkling.

She pulled me close, her hands sliding up my back. She kissed me, her lips soft and warm against mine. I felt a jolt of desire low in my belly as she deepened the kiss, her tongue probing my mouth.

I tangled my fingers in her hair, pulling her closer.

"You're really not going to tell me where we're going next?" I asked, pouting my lips slightly.

"Not even a hint," she replied with a peck. "Now, get dressed. The car is ready downstairs, and we don't want to keep Raul waiting."

Fifteen minutes later, we were in the car.

―――――

As we were driving, I couldn't help but wonder what else Spencer had planned for the evening. I was completely taken aback by how amazing the date had been so far. I had never experienced anything like it before.

We arrived at a bowling alley, and Spencer led me inside. She had rented out the whole place, and we were the only ones there. It was a bit strange, but also kind of exciting.

"I thought we could have some fun here," she explained. "Bowling is a blast."

"It sounds like it," I agreed.

She walked over to the bowling balls and selected one for me. She handed it to me, and I was surprised by how heavy it was.

She helped me put on my bowling shoes and led me over to the lane.

"Let me help you," she said, coming up behind me.

She guided me through the motions of bowling, her hands gently touching me as she showed me how to swing the ball. I couldn't help but feel a rush of desire as she wrapped her arms around me. She was so close I could smell her perfume, a subtle scent that was intoxicating.

I took a deep breath and focused on the pins at the end of the lane. I swung the ball, letting it go at just the right moment. It rolled down the lane and hit the pins, knocking them all down.

"Nicely done," Spencer said, smiling at me.

I turned to look at her, and our eyes met. There was a spark between us, a connection that I couldn't deny.

I was drawn to her in a way that I couldn't explain. I felt like I had known her for years, even though we had only just met. She seemed familiar to me, like an old friend.

I walked over to the ball return, trying to get my bearings. My heart was racing, and I felt a little lightheaded. I needed to calm down and focus on the game.

After a few frames, we were both in the zone. She was laughing, and I was actually keeping up with her.

After a few frames, we were both in the zone. She was laughing, and I was actually keeping up with her.

"So, tell me more about your childhood," I asked as she sunk another strike.

"Not much to tell, really," she said with a shrug.

"There has to be more than that," I insisted as she walked up to the ball return.

She paused for a moment before bowling her round. It wasn't until she turned back towards me that she began to speak, earnestly and freely.

"When I was younger, we had this huge farmhouse on my grandparents' farm. It was the perfect place to be a kid. We had all sorts of animals to care for, and my parents would let me take the horses out for a ride every once in a while," Spencer started, the words flowing freely but softly.

I'd never heard her talk so openly about her past, and it was refreshing. I stayed silent and let her continue.

"I was super shy when I was young, and my parents worried about me not having many friends. But I didn't mind it at all. I spent most of my days reading books in the barn or exploring the fields. Summers were always my favorite season because I got to spend it all out there."

She paused as a soft smile spread over her face at the memory. It was adorable seeing her open up like this. She looked like a kid again, telling these stories from childhood.

I couldn't stop staring at her. Watching her. Observing her in this tender moment.

My eyes were glued to her.

Spencer came over and stood next to me, her arm brushing against mine. I shivered, a tingle running down my spine.

"Are you okay, Lauren?" she asked, her voice with a touch of concern.

"I'm fine," I managed to croak out. "I just...really liked hearing you tell that story."

I looked up at her and was surprised to see a glint of amusement in her eyes. She was enjoying this.

"Do you need a minute?" she asked, her voice low and husky.

I nodded, unable to speak. She reached out and touched my cheek, her fingers softly caressing my skin. I closed my eyes, savoring the feeling of her touch.

"Lauren?" Her voice was soft, but insistent.

"Hmmm?" I murmured.

"Look at me."

That had become her line for the night, and I loved it.

Fuck, I think I loved her.

I opened my eyes and met her gaze. Her eyes were dark with desire, and I felt a jolt of heat deep in my belly. She leaned down and brushed her lips against mine, sending shivers of pleasure through my body.

I closed my eyes and leaned into her kiss, my body responding to her touch.

Her arms wrapped around me, pulling me closer, and I could feel the heat of her skin through her clothes. I ran my hands up her back, tangling my fingers in her hair. I felt like I couldn't get close enough to her.

The tension between us was electric, and I felt a surge of desire low in my belly.

She pulled away, leaving me breathless and wanting more.

"Are you ready to bowl now?" she asked, her voice husky.

"Yes," I breathed, my voice trembling slightly.

I was aching for her, but I knew we had to finish the game first.

I walked over to the ball return, and Spencer followed. I picked up my ball and tried to focus on the pins at the end of the lane. My hands were shaking as I lined up my shot. I took a deep breath and swung the ball, letting it go at just the right moment. It rolled down the lane and hit the pins, knocking them all down.

I turned to Spencer and grinned. "Strike!"

"Good job," she said, smiling at me.

I walked over to her and stood in front of her, our bodies inches apart.

"I think I'm starting to get the hang of this," I whispered, looking up at her.

She reached out and cupped my cheek in her palm. "You're a quick learner."

I closed my eyes and leaned into her touch, savoring the feeling of her skin against mine.

"You make me feel things I've never felt before," I breathed, my voice trembling slightly.

She leaned down and brushed her lips against mine, sending shivers of pleasure through my body.

I closed my eyes and kissed her back, my body responding to her touch.

Her arms wrapped around me, pulling me closer, and I could feel the heat of her skin through her clothes. I ran my hands up her back, tangling my fingers in her hair. I felt like I couldn't get close enough to her.

The tension between us was electric, and I felt a surge of desire low in my belly.

She pulled away, leaving me breathless and wanting more.

"What do ya say we head back to the hotel after this game?" she asked, running her thumb over my brow.

"Whatdaya say we assume that you're going to kick my ass once again and just head back now?" I whispered.

"Grab your things and let's go, babe," she grinned with a kiss.

21

We returned to the hotel after bowling, and Spencer led me up to her suite in hot silence. Without a word, she unlocked the door and ushered me inside.

I wandered over to the windows and looked out at the city skyline below. The view was breathtaking, and I couldn't help but smile when I thought about just how nervous I had been just a few weeks ago when I looked out at this view for the first time. So much had changed in just a month.

I felt a hand on my shoulder, and Spencer appeared next to me, drinks in hand. She slipped her arms around my waist and rested her chin on my shoulder.

"Beautiful, isn't it?" she murmured.

"Yes, it is," I breathed, my voice barely above a whisper.

I turned in her arms and looked up at her. She was smiling at me, her eyes sparkling with mischief.

"So, what are you thinking, Miss Wolf?" I asked.

"I was thinking that we have some unfinished business," Spencer murmured, her lips brushing against mine.

I sighed and melted into her kiss. It was a deep, passionate kiss that left me breathless. I clung to her, my nails digging into her shoulders as she deepened the kiss. Her hands roamed my body, her fingers gently stroking my skin.

"Oh, God," I moaned, feeling myself falling deeper and deeper for her.

She broke the kiss and pulled away slightly, her eyes filled with desire.

"Lauren," she breathed, her voice husky. "You make me feel things I've never felt before."

I stared up at her, my heart pounding in my chest.

"You make me feel alive, Lauren."

I swallowed hard, my mouth suddenly dry.

She took a step towards me, closing the distance between us.

"Tell me you feel the same," she whispered, her voice trembling slightly.

I opened my mouth to respond, but no words came out.

She reached out and cupped my cheek in her palm.

"Please, Lauren."

I nodded, unable to speak.

She leaned down and brushed her lips against mine, sending a shiver of pleasure through my body. She trailed kisses along my jawline, her tongue gently tracing the outline of my ear.

"You taste so good," she murmured, her voice sending shivers down my spine.

She ran her fingers through my hair, her nails lightly scratching my scalp.

I sighed, leaning into her touch. I felt myself giving in to her, my body responding to her every whim.

"Oh, Lauren," she breathed, her voice low and husky. "I want you. I want to be inside you. I want to make you come. Over and over again. For so, so long. I think I'm falling in love with you."

I gasped, my eyes flying open. I stared up at her, my heart pounding in my chest.

"Are you sure?" I whispered, hardly daring to breathe.

She nodded, her eyes never leaving mine.

I reached up and stroked her cheek, my fingers tracing the contours of her face.

"Make love to me, Spencer," I murmured.

She groaned, her eyes closing as she savored the sensation of my touch.

"Open your eyes, Spencer. Look at me," I commanded.

She opened her eyes and gazed down at me, her pupils dilated with desire.

"I want to see you, Spencer. I want to watch you lose control."

"Lauren..." she whispered, her voice trembling with emotion.

I pulled her down to me, my lips crashing against hers in a desperate kiss.

Her tongue invaded my mouth, exploring every inch. She tasted like sin and salvation, and I couldn't get enough.

My hands tangled in her hair, pulling her closer. I needed her, all of her.

"Oh, God, Lauren," she moaned, her hands gripping my hips.

"Please, Spencer," I begged, my body aching for her.

"Are you sure?" she asked, her voice barely above a whisper.

"Yes," I gasped, my eyes fluttering closed. "Please, Spencer."

She kissed me again, her hands roaming my body. I felt her fingers tracing the curves of my breasts, my stomach, my hips.

I moaned, arching my back, pressing myself against her.

She trailed kisses down my neck, her lips soft and warm against my skin.

I tangled my fingers in her hair, pulling her closer.

Her hand slid between my legs, gently stroking me. I was already wet, aching for her touch.

"Oh, Spencer," I moaned, my hips bucking against her.

She continued to stroke me, her fingers sliding easily over my wetness. I was panting, desperate for release.

"Please," I gasped, my nails digging into her shoulders.

"What do you want, Lauren?" she breathed, her voice husky with desire.

"I need you, Spencer. Please."

"Tell me," she insisted.

"I need you inside me, Spencer. Please."

She moaned, her eyes dark with desire. She shifted her position, slipping two fingers inside me.

"Oh, God," I cried, my hips bucking against her hand.

She pumped her fingers in and out of me, curling them up to hit the sweet spot that made my head spin.

"More," I begged, my voice trembling with need.

She slipped a third finger inside me, stretching me.

"Come for me, Lauren," she commanded, her voice low and husky.

My body trembled, my back arching off the bed. I clung to her, my nails digging into her shoulders as my orgasm washed over me, wave after wave of pleasure crashing through me.

"Oh, Spencer," I cried, my body convulsing.

"That's it," she murmured, her voice soothing as I rode out the last aftershocks.

I collapsed against the mattress, utterly spent. My heart was racing, and my skin was covered in a fine sheen of sweat.

"Good Lord, you're beautiful," Spencer breathed, her eyes never leaving mine.

She slid her fingers out of me and licked them, her eyes rolling back in her head as she tasted me.

"And you're delicious."

She leaned down and kissed me, her lips soft and warm against mine.

"Thank you," I murmured, my eyes fluttering closed.

I was utterly exhausted. I'd had three intense orgasms in the space of a few hours. And we'd barely even begun our evening.

Spencer propped herself up on one elbow and smiled down at me, her fingers tracing lazy circles on my belly.

"No, thank you," she replied.

I chuckled. "Why are you thanking me?"

"For letting me do this," she said, her voice low and husky. "I'm not finished with you yet, either."

"I'm sure you aren't," I smirked. "I can feel how aroused you still are."

"And it's all your fault," she growled, her teeth grazing my earlobe.

I shivered, my body aching for more.

"Let's get something to eat," she suggested.

I blinked up at her, surprised.

"Eat?"

"Yes," she said, chuckling. "You know, fuel."

"Right," I agreed. "Food."

She laughed.

"Come on," she said, standing and reaching for her robe. "Let's order some room service for a late night snack."

"Okay," I said. We walked over to the phone, and Spencer picked up the menu.

"What would you like?" she asked.

"Hmmm, I think I'll have a burger and fries," I said. "That

sounds like the perfect second-dinner ending to a night of bowling.

"Good choice." She smiled.

"What about you?"

"I'll have the same," she said, grinning.

"So, you have a chef who prepares everything here?" I asked.

"Yes, I just ring down to the front desk, and I can order whatever I'd like," she explained. It was moments like this that I remembered just how different our worlds were.

"So, the paparazzi are going to be following you around even more now, huh? When the movie is over and you have to go back home?" I inquired, changing the subject.

"Yeah, I guess." She shrugged. "It comes with the territory."

"I can't believe you've been through this your whole life."

"Pretty much," she sighed. "It's gotten a lot worse over the past couple years, though."

"Wow," I breathed, shaking my head.

"You get used to it," she said. "After a while, you stop seeing them."

"How?"

"It takes a lot of practice," she said, chuckling.

"That's good to know," I murmured.

"So, we should talk about this past weekend. The damn pictures and headlines. The marketing team really hit it out of the ballpark on getting the 'story' out there."

"They did a great job," I said, trying to hide the mild frustration I still felt about the media storm around Spencer and Chris' weekend in New York.

"It wasn't my idea, but it worked." She frowned. "And now, the paparazzi are going to be following me around more than ever. They're likely going to try and grab some snaps of you too. They throw a wide net."

"Really?" I squeaked.

"Yes, so you might want to stay with me for a bit...until we're done filming." She quickly took a sip of her drink.

"Stay with you? In your suite?"

"Yes," she said, smiling.

"What about Allie and my apartment?"

"We can make arrangements for someone to grab whatever you need," she suggested. "And of course you'd keep your apartment. I just figured it might be easier this way."

I frowned, considering. It would be nice to spend more time with Spencer, but I wasn't sure I was ready to uproot my life completely.

"Let me think about it," I murmured.

"Fair enough," she agreed. "Now, let's eat."

She dialed the number for room service and ordered two burgers and fries.

"Twenty minutes," she announced, hanging up the phone.

"Perfect." I grinned.

We curled up on the sofa together, and Spencer wrapped her arms around me, holding me close.

"You're not cold, are you?"

"No, not with you next to me," I whispered.

She kissed the top of my head, and I snuggled closer.

"Tell me about growing up in Seattle," she requested.

"What do you want to know?"

"Did you go to public school? How many siblings do you have? Where are your parents now? Do you miss your childhood home?"

"Wow, that's a lot of questions."

She laughed. "Sorry, I'm just curious."

"It's fine." I smiled. "Well, I grew up in an old neighborhood. Our house was a bit shabby, but it had lots of charm and history. It was always full of books and music."

"That must have been nice," she murmured. I nodded, observing her sudden wistfulness. "So, how was your weekend, really? We never had a proper chance to talk after the media got crazy."

"I got drunk and cried a lot," I chuckled darkly. It was true. It had been a much more difficult weekend than I was expecting.

"And I thought my weekend was bad," Spencer sighed. "Tell me about it, babe. What was troubling you?"

"There's not much to tell. It was pretty awful. I missed you, and I was worried about you," I whispered.

"Aww, you were worried about me?" she asked with a slight grin.

"Of course I was!" I laughed. "Out all night with Chris King's hands all over you. It made me a little nervous. Or maybe jealous. It made me feel something."

"You didn't need to be. I was fine. More bored than anything. Chris isn't exactly an intellectual," she chuckled.

"It was just much weirder than I was expecting, seeing you on a date with him. Having my friends see it too and not knowing how to respond. Having to read all of those damn social media comments. It just got to me for a moment."

"But it's an act. A charade. A fiction. You know that, and I've told you so. I'm not interested in him, in any shape or form. And I'd certainly never have sex with him. Never. The thought is abhorrent. That man is a pig. An entitled, arrogant, womanizing, spoiled, self-centered, chauvinistic pig." She shudders, her face creasing with revulsion.

"Yes, I understand that," I nodded.

"But...it doesn't make you feel any better, does it?" She asked sympathetically. She reached her hand across and grabbed mine.

"Not much," I confessed.

"Okay, then let's think of some ways we can make this

work. Because unfortunately, it's part of my job, but I want you. Desperately. And I don't want my work to hurt you."

"What did you have in mind?" I murmured, hardly daring to breathe.

"Well," she said, tracing small circles on the back of my hand with her thumb. "I still need to give the impression that Chris and I are seeing each other. At least until the movie premiere and my contract expires. But, that doesn't mean you couldn't be waiting for me at home when I get done with my few obligations in the interim."

"Home?" I asked, my voice shaking.

"Yeah," she smiled. "I'll be finished with filming here by end of next week. After that, I'll probably be heading back to LA. What if you join me?"

"What do you mean?" I whispered.

"Come home with me. To LA."

"You're kidding, right?"

"Why would I kid about something like that?"

"Um...because that would be insane."

"I'm a very private person, Lauren. I'm not going to be making a public spectacle of us, and the only people I associate with in Los Angeles are people who care about me and who have no desire to see me hurt. Plus, if you're there, you'll be able to avoid the press. There are plenty of places to hide."

"And how would I live?"

"I would take care of everything," she replied, dismissively. "Just think about it, Lauren."

"It's a bit sudden, don't you think? I have an apartment, and I have a life."

"Think how much easier it would be for you to work and for you to have a life if you could focus on doing whatever you want to do. Write. Read. Edit. Whatever it is you actually want to focus on. Besides, we could see each other every day, and you'd have complete privacy. You could stay at the house, or you could find an apartment."

"You'd trust me to do that?"

"You can do whatever you want. But I do have to admit, I'd much prefer you in my home.."

"I don't know."

"What's the alternative, Lauren?"

"I could stay here."

"What's the fun in that?" she pouted. "Don't answer that," she added, seeing my hesitant reaction.

She was right. What was the fun in staying here? I'd graduated. I hadn't had any real prospects here until Spencer and the film had walked into my life.

And, as much as I would miss living with my friends, we were all starting to move on to the next chapter in our lives.

Was this mine?

Could Spencer be part of my next life?

"Lauren?"

"I'm not sure."

"Don't be scared," she murmured, and her words echoed my thoughts from earlier.

"I'm not...much."

"Good," she whispered, kissing me softly on the lips. "I was really missing you too, this weekend."

"Oh, yeah?" I smiled. "What did you miss?"

"Talking to you. Seeing you. Being near you. Your laugh. Your smile." She ran the bridge of her nose across the curve of my jaw. "And how did I make you feel, being so far away?"

"Lots of ways," I muttered, starting to lose my train of thought in her intoxicating presence.

"Tell me."

"Like now, lying here on the couch with you, talking and laughing. When you smile, you make me feel so alive, so connected. It's the oddest feeling. I've never felt like this before."

"Hmm," she murmured, and kissed my temple.

"And then the sex..." I whispered.

"Is very good."

"It is. I've never had anything even close," I sighed into her lips.

"So. So. Good." Her eyes fluttered closed under heavy lids. She was tired, and it was absolutely adorable seeing her fight off sleep.

There was a knock on the door and a call of "Room Service" from the other side. I slipped out of Spencer's tired arms and accepted the food. Rather than set it out, I wrapped it up and stuck it in the fridge for morning.

Spencer rose from her curled up position on the couch with a yawn. "Was that the food?"

"Yeah, I put it away for breakfast. Let's go to bed," I suggested.

She nodded, led me into the bedroom, and I slipped under the covers. She climbed in beside me and switched off the lamp.

"Come here," she whispered.

"Mmmm." I snuggled against her. She wrapped her arms around me, and we lay, curled together in silence.

"Lauren?" she said softly.

"Hmm?"

"I'm so glad you're here. It's been a shitty weekend without you."

"Mine, too," I whispered, my lips against her chest. "Good night, Spencer."

"Good night, sweetheart."

I fell asleep in her arms, and she was still holding me when I woke in the morning.

22

WHEN I WOKE the next morning, I was alone in the big bed. I stretched in the silk sheets, feeling a delicious ache between my thighs.

Damn. We really had an active evening.

Spencer was nowhere to be seen. I checked my watch. It was eight in the morning. I found her note propped up on the pillows.

GOOD MORNING, *baby.*
  I hope you slept well.
  Took a call. Back soon.
  x S x

OH, so she'd started calling me "baby." I liked it. I'd never had a real pet-name with anyone before.

I was pleasantly sore, and the ache was welcome, a reminder of her long, piano fingers and her strong tongue. She was more than I could have imagined. And she clearly wanted to be with me.

So, why had I been such a coward last night?

Why had I changed the subject when she had asked me to come be with her in LA?

When I really thought about it, that's all I really wanted.

The door at the front of the suite opened, and Spencer strode in, her ear-pods in and a handful of coffee and pastries.

"Morning, sleepyhead," she grinned. "Sorry I wasn't here when you woke up."

"It's okay. How did your call go?"

"Fine." She shrugged. "Business as usual. Rebecca's getting all the arrangements for me to get back to LA. It takes more work than most realize, all this relocating back and forth."

I nodded and sat down next to her on the couch as she laid out the drinks and pastries on the coffee table.

"Speaking of LA..." I started, reaching out for her hand.

"Oh, fuck. I totally blew it last night by bringing it up, didn't I?!" Spencer exclaimed, clearly still upset from the night before. "I rushed it, didn't I? Uhhh, I just got so nervous."

"No, no!" I assured her. "You didn't rush anything. I was just nervous myself. I still don't know how to handle all of this. I just needed a minute to think. But I have, and I want to come to LA with you."

"You do?!" she exclaimed.

"Yes, Spencer. I'd like nothing more."

She threw her arms around me and crushed me to her, burying her face in my neck.

"Oh, thank God," she breathed.

"You're welcome," I said. "And I'm sorry. You know, for last night. I didn't handle it as well as I should have."

"It's okay," she murmured, kissing me tenderly. "We're all on edge, I think."

"Yes, I think you're right," I agreed. "I'm just glad we could work through this together. Makes things a hell of a lot easier."

"We'll get it sorted," she promised with a confident smile.

"So, when will we leave?"

"Well, I need to be on set until filming wraps at the end of next week. Rebecca is sorting out the move back, and she can help take over any moving help you might need," Spencer replied. Taking a moment's pause, she finally continued, "So, are you sure you're ready for this? It's a big step. And I've never lived with anyone. You'll have to tell me what you need. I have no idea."

"You'll have to tell me, too," I smiled.

"We can buy anything we need. My house is very sparse as is. I was really going for minimalism when I last designed."

"You?" I asked, astonished. "Minimal?"

She nodded with a sly smile.

"I guess we have a lot to learn about each other."

"We're going to have to keep up appearances, though, you know," she sighed.

"How so?"

"Well, the public can't know we're together."

I felt my face fall slightly, but I tried my best to hide any disappointment. I understood why we had to remain a private relationship, but it bummed me out nonetheless. "I know. I know."

"I'm really sorry, Lauren, I just have a career to think about. My reputation. I have an image, and it's important to keep it on brand if I want to keep working. You'll just have to trust me on this. Can you do that?"

"I trust you, Spencer. I know you have your reasons. But you can't blame a girl for trying."

"So, what's going to happen now?"

"We need to start making plans. If you're going to LA with me, I need to know exactly what your needs and desires are."

"My needs and desires?"

"Yes, my dear." She smiled. "Now, sit up."

"Oh, this should be interesting," I said, smirking at her.

She raised her eyebrows at me, and her eyes flashed with mischievous excitement.

"Sit. Up."

I did as she asked, sitting on the sofa, legs splayed slightly. She had something in mind, and I couldn't wait to see what it was.

She left the room, and I heard her rummaging around in her closet. What was she up to?

She returned with a large suitcase, which she set down in front of me. She popped it open and pulled out a key.

"Here's a key to the front door," she said, pressing it into my palm.

Her words were soft yet firm—like velvet wrapped steel wire —and held power over mine completely. Her lips curled upward ever subtly. She looked beautiful, and entirely sure.

Something about her confidence made me realize this was absolutely the right choice. I wanted to be with her, and we could totally make this work.

"How did you already have this made?" I asked, turning the metal over in my hand.

"Let's just say I had a hopeful hunch," she smiled. "Half of me figured that if I went ahead and made you a key, it would be a bit like manifesting you coming home with me."

"That is very 'LA' of you," I laughed. "But also so damn adorable."

"You're going to have to get used to some 'LA,' witchy-bitchy shit," Spencer chuckled.

"What will I tell people here, Spence?" I asked, looking down at the key in my palm.

"Tell them whatever you like."

"But, they're my friends. I wouldn't want to be dishonest with them."

"Then tell them the truth, that I asked you to come to LA."

"It's that simple?"

"For you, yes," she whispered. "It's easy: everyone already knows that we've been working together. They're just going to assume that I hired you on full-time after the movie ends. All we have to do is lean in to that assumption. No one has to know the real reason you're constantly by my side."

"Sounds like a plan to me," I nodded in agreement. It wasn't ideal, but it allowed us freedom and privacy that wouldn't be possible if we were open about the truth.

23

I DROVE BACK to my apartment the next morning with the weirdest mixture of excitement for the future and a heavy heart knowing that I would have to tell my friends I was leaving. And, honestly, I was nervous. I wasn't sure how they would react.

Moving to LA with Spencer was life-changing news.

When I arrived at the apartment, I found my two friends sitting around the kitchen table. Allie was on the phone, no doubt talking to one of her med school classmates. Julie was tapping away at her laptop and was sipping a huge mug of coffee.

"Well, look who's back," Julie teased when I walked in. "Come have a seat."

I made myself a cup of coffee, took a deep breath, and sat down between my two friends. The apartment seemed so still and quiet as the three of us gazed at one another. I decided I needed to just dive right in. There was no sense in dragging this out any longer than necessary.

I watched my best friends' faces as I told them about my past-night. I wasn't sure how to begin, so I simply started by saying:

"Spencer Wolf and I are going to LA next week, together. She's invited me to stay with her, so I'll be moving there."

They both just looked at me like I had gone insane. And then Allie said the first words that anyone had spoken.

"Okay, I'll bite. Start over."

"What do you mean?"

"I've never seen you this happy, Lauren," Allie explained. "I mean, ever. So, while I've been cautiously opposed to the idea of you dating a movie star, if it turns you into the Lauren you were before all this worry started, I'm all for it."

"Thank you," I breathed, my shoulders sagging in relief.

"Yeah," Julie chimed in. "Honestly, we've been concerned you've changed after the last couple of months before you landed this assistant gig. I haven't liked it. Seeing you happy again is always a gift."

"So, you're okay if I go off to LA with Spencer and leave you two on your own for a while?"

"Of course we are!" my friends exclaimed in unison.

"You have your own amazing vibe to take over the space," I reassured her. "Besides, how many times have you complained about how cramped this apartment is?"

"Um, a lot," she smirked.

"You'll have some space, then."

"I'm just glad you're finally with her. That you can be yourself with her and still feel comfortable in your relationship. It really is what you deserve."

I paused and took a deep breath. "So, what do you guys really think? Is this crazy?"

"I don't know," Allie said. "Do you have to go?"

"Well, yeah," I replied, suddenly entirely sure of my answer. "This feels like the next step. It feels right."

"Then, I suppose you do," she replied, dejectedly. "So, we're going to go back to having Saturday night dinners, only there won't be you around to cook them?"

"Not me, no," I said, grimacing. "But maybe we can give you the phone numbers of some professionals you can call in to make the meals."

Julie smacked me on the arm.

"Come on," she groaned.

"Come on," she groaned. "You're gonna miss us, aren't you?"

"Hell yes, I'm going to miss you. You're my family, and now I'm being forced to choose between you and my dream, and I hate it."

My eyes welled with tears. Julie put her arms around me.

"Oh honey, don't cry," she whispered, rubbing my back. "I mean, I was being sarcastic, but I didn't expect to make you cry."

"It's okay," I choked out between tears. "I'm just really, really torn. I've got to go. This is what I want. And it's not forever. Just until we get things sorted out. Until we have more information on what the hell we're doing. I don't know."

I buried my face in Julie's shoulder, and she held me as I sobbed. After a while, my tears subsided, and she stroked my hair.

Allie was sitting across the table, watching us, her eyes filled with a mixture of sadness and happiness.

"So, how long are you gone for?"

"As long as I need to be," I murmured.

"And what happens to our apartment?"

"I'll find a subletter who will cover the rent."

"Will they be a lesbian?" Julie asked, a hint of sadness in her tone.

"I doubt it," I chuckled weakly. "The market is much better for straight girls."

"That's unfortunate," Julie murmured.

"I'm sorry," I said.

"Don't be," Allie said, standing up and brushing her palms off. "If it wasn't for the fact that I had to fucking study, I'd take you both out for drinks at Maggie's. Can you two handle one more ladies night?"

"Maggie's Margs!?" I exclaimed.

"No, asshole," she chuckled, sticking her tongue out at me. "A proper farewell celebration. Dinner and fancy dress attire and cocktails with ingredients we have to google."

"Sure," I smiled.

"Glorious."

"Maybe we can invite Spencer too?" Allie suggested. "It would be nice to actually meet the woman who is stealing our friend before you all leave."

"Definitely," I nodded. It was weird that my friends hadn't even met the woman I was moving halfway across the country with. "I'll call her and we can set up a whole 'meet the friends' brunch. I know she'd love that. She's been asking about you all."

"Asked about us?!" Julie exclaimed. "That means Spencer freaking Wolf knows who we are!"

"Of course she does, silly," I smiled. "I told her all about my lovely friends."

"Well it is settled then," Julie declared. "We are having one final farewell evening to send you off properly!"

———

As I CRAWLED into my own bed for the first time that week, I was suddenly hyper aware of the lack of Spencer in my arms. I missed her, and it had only been day apart.

Reaching for my phone, I smiled seeing that I'd missed a message from Spencer: 'Thinking of you. Give me a ring if you have time before you fall asleep.'

I didn't need much more motivation. My fingers found her contact and hit call without a second thought.

The sound of her voice sent a shiver down my spine.

"Hey you," she murmured.

"I miss you," I blurted.

She chuckled. "I miss you, too. So, how did telling your friends go? Did they take the news well?"

"They were totally fine with it. They want me to be happy. I mean, they love me, and so it feels like they know when I say something like that, I have thought about it. Julie seemed a little sad, maybe, like things will change, but I think she's just worried, you know?"

"A little, yeah. Because my life is still kind of amazing, but it's definitely not what you'd call 'normal.'"

I laughed.

"I bet it's not. Speaking of normal, the girls want to have one last dinner night out together at our favorite spot. A farewell dinner sorta thing. And I was wondering if you would join us?"

Spencer paused for a moment, and I could hear her thinking.

"It would mean the world to me," I blurted out, hoping to use my sympathetic girlfriend card.

"Oh, you are simply asking for trouble by pulling out the pity card. Trouble with a capital T."

"Does that mean yes?" I grinned.

"Yes, I'll be there. But I reserve the right to book out a private room at the restaurant. That way we can all get to know each other without the fear of camera phones or paps."

"That sounds wonderful," I grinned. The thought of all of my favorite women in one room made me giddy.

"Alright, well it's probably both of our bed times. My first scene is scheduled for noon tomorrow, and we can probably both use some rest."

"Alright," I sighed. "I'll miss falling asleep next to you, but I'll see you tomorrow."

"Sweet dreams, my dear," she hummed through the phone.

"You too."

"Sleep tight," Spencer said. "I'll see you tomorrow. Love you."

"Love you, too," I replied, feeling warm and fuzzy inside.

Even though this "relationship" was entirely new to both of us, we both knew that this was something neither of us was ready to let go of.

24

FRIDAY CAME in the blink of an eye, and so too did our scheduled 'Ladies' Night.'

Since she was coming off a long day of high glam marketing interviews and photo shoots with Chris, Spencer and I had already planned to arrive separately. She also didn't want to scare Julie and Allie by showing up intimidatingly together. It was far better for me to get ready with my already nervous friends, and I knew that the last thing they needed was to be greeted and harassed by paparazzi that might be trailing her car if we all rode together.

The paps loved a good 'girl's night out' shot.

Spencer texted me as she was on her way to the restaurant, saying that she'd be there in five minutes. In the meantime, Julie and Allie watched me nervously as I stared at the door, waiting for her to arrive.

As I ran my tongue across my teeth, Allie finally asked:

"Are you sure we don't have to wear, like, whatever the female equivalent of 'black tie' is? Because I don't have the wardrobe for that. Or the money for a super wild dinner. My budget is, like, nonexistent. And my fancy dinner skills are severely lacking."

"Stop it," I snapped, rolling my eyes at her. "You don't need to do anything. Just behave like a human being, and it will be fine. Plus, you know Spencer is going to pick up the bill. Hell, she hired the entire private dining room just for us."

"Okay, okay," she let out an anxious breath. "I'm just a little nervous."

"Just relax, ok? You've had a drink, we've all had a drink. Just enjoy yourself, it will be great."

"Fine." Allie sighed heavily.

"It's going to be fantastic." I stated in a comforting voice, giving her a quick hug.

Just as I glanced up one final time, the restaurant doors opened and in walked Spencer. My jaw nearly dropped with how gorgeous she looked tonight.

Of course, I was well aware that I was biased; my beautiful girlfriend wore the same gorgeous grin she always did. She approached the table casually, her eyes narrowed and then brightened as she realized I had pulled out the chair that was now waiting for her. After strutting elegantly through the room, she draped herself across the comfortable, plush chair in a typical relaxed position for her.

Reaching for my hand, she gave me a quick peck on the cheek as she sat down beside me at the circular table. To my left sat Allie and Julie, while to my right, was Spencer. All of my favorite people gathered together made my heart swell with love.

Spencer's fingertips immediately started roaming over my wrist, as she chatted happily and exchanged pleasantries with Julie and Allie. To everyone else at the table, it seemed like a completely natural, relaxed atmosphere. But inside my chest, I could hear the thrumming of my pulse as her soft, gentle touches excited me.

This was the first time we'd gotten to be a couple in front

of anyone other than Rebecca, and it was stirring something wonderful inside of my chest.

I watched as her gaze flitted along the menus made for us, absorbing all of the options available from whatever famous chef was running this beautiful kitchen. In this change of scenery, she seemed like an entirely different person. Though she was dressed in an absolutely adorable dress, she exuded an odd mixture of nerves, excitement, and calmness. It's the nerves and excitement that were amplifying her natural beauty.

In fact, to my eyes, she was the most beautiful woman I'd ever seen, hands down.

Her red lipstick matched the same red dress she wore, and the fabric seemed to wrap around her body like a glove. Every part of her, from the curve of her spine to the lean shape of her arms, to the smooth, sexy plumpness of her gorgeous, long legs was perfectly accentuated. And she owned it so effortlessly.

"So, what does a day in your life look like, Spencer?" Allie asked, a bit loudly, interrupting my ogling session.

Spencer turned her attention towards Allie and started describing her average day as I leaned in closer to her body, resting my head gently on her shoulder. The skin to skin contact felt good, and I closed my eyes, enjoying every second of it. I was getting hot, a sign that I was either nervous or horny. It was likely both.

As I opened my eyes, I saw Julie watching us intently from across the table, and I wondered briefly if my friend was judging my blatant public display of affection towards Spencer. After a few seconds of holding contact with her unreadable gaze, Julie just smiled, seeming to enjoy watching me happy, and was immediately re-absorbed in one of Spencer's fascinating stories about travel or some mishap on set.

I honestly wasn't paying close attention.
I was a little buzzed.
And a lot enamored.

The room faded into a dull murmur as I gazed lovingly at Spencer. She hadn't been drinking like the rest of us, but it didn't seem to faze her one bit. In fact, I felt like she was over-compensating for her calm sobriety by being overly nice and extremely complimentary to my tipsy, star-struck friends. Under the table, I caught Spencer's hand between my legs and gently squeezed it to get her attention.

With a sheepish grin, she twisted her head slightly, an amused expression appearing on her face. "What?"

"Thanks," I grinned, "for being so nice."

"Nice?" Spencer chuckled, leaning closer. "Is there anything else I should be?"

"No. I'm not complaining, but just—"

Spencer cut me off with a wink.

"Remember what I said before, baby." She murmured into my ear. "Things are changing after filming. There's a huge adjustment period, so I want to make sure your friends approve of the actress from LA who swooped in and plucked their bestie away on a whirlwind romance. I have to be on my especially best behavior in front of your friends."

"Well, then you're being an incredibly good sport."

Before I had a chance to get by any more flustered over Spencer's oozing charm, the food thankfully arrived and brought the conversation back to the table.

"So, Spencer," Julie started, "what's going on with all of these paparazzi pictures of you and Chris King?"

Spencer casually speared another bite of salad, rolling her eyes, obviously trying to figure out how to handle the situation diplomatically.

"That's just a PR and marketing thing," she said with a sigh.

"Do you see those two a lot while you're filming?"

She just shrugged in response.

"Who?" Allie asked, chiming in.

Chris King, that sexy guy Spencer's been seen with and her alleged 'special' friend. That doesn't answer my question. Your media team seems to be gearing up for something with you two, and there are rumors flying about that you have something going on."

"Because they do their jobs and this is what the studio paid them for," I replied, stepping in to save Spencer from this uncomfortable line of questioning. I couldn't tell what had gotten into Julie, but she was acting defensive suddenly.

"So, there's nothing going on there?" Julie continued, digging further.

"Yep," Spencer chortled through a mouthful of spaghetti, "who doesn't like some good, old fashioned male bonding time with Chris. Get your head outta the gutter."

I had to suppress a smirk at her comments, and I felt the sharp tickle of a snort forming in my nasal cavity. Realizing how odd Spencer sounded, I shifted awkwardly in my seat, attempting to adjust myself.

Once Spencer had recovered, she turned her attention toward Allie and promptly tried engaging her in conversation.

Spencer had been playing the role of the Hollywood A-lister since I'd known her, so it was second nature for me to observe, but I knew this would likely be my friend's only glimpse of the woman I loved before we moved across the country to keep dating. Luckily for her, Spencer happened to be beautiful and confident, with killer human instincts, both on and off the screen. Even the way she threw around casual compliments and shared interesting anecdotes seemed sincere and refreshing.

It didn't take her long to completely charm Julie and Allie, distracting us with her natural charm and impeccable mannerisms. She was a true professional, but she was so natural, and down to earth. I couldn't help but fall in love with her, all over again.

Once the conversation had found a steady rhythm, Spencer finally relaxed into the chair. And as she sat and chatted with my friends, the air seemed to flow smoothly through her body. She simply sipped her water quietly as we all laughed at her stories.

I watched the way Allie's eyes lit up every time Spencer would find a way to segue back to the topic of chemistry, and the way Julie would tilt her head in awe every time she would start a story, letting Spencer have her moment to shine and bask in all of the attention.

At the beginning of dinner, Spencer had ordered herself a glass of wine, but had barely touched it since the first sip. Instead, she proceeded to carry the discussion throughout the entire meal, talking constantly and answering any questions we could throw at her.

The whole time, the charming smile remained on her face. It seemed to spread through her entire being, leaving little to be desired. The way her skin glowed was absolutely mesmerizing, as her pearly white teeth flashed and sparkled brightly under the soft lighting. The vibrant, full smile only added to her already captivating appearance.

It was the first time I'd seen her seem so comfortable around strangers.

Maybe it was because the other women were being very casual, and had finally settled into relaxed fun. Whatever it was, Spencer was enjoying herself immensely, and it had an effect on all three of us.

The way Spencer carried herself was almost regal. She

commanded an atmosphere of power and self-assurance, completely secure in herself. I felt a strange sensation inside, that pulled my heart and stomach towards her.

I'm not sure what it was, but it was becoming stronger by the day.

25

ALL TOO SOON, the evening began drawing to a close.

Spencer reached across the table, collecting the check and handed her black Amex to the waitress with a sly wink. "I thought I'd get the tab on my farewell treat."

We walked through the restaurant to the front door together, chatting amiably the entire way, and emerged into the brisk evening air of the private back parking lot together.

After hugging my two friends goodbye, and making our way to Spencer's driver, I quickly dove through the car door, scrambling behind Spencer, and immediately felt her arm pull me into her warm, sweet smelling body.

Breathing her in, I sighed contentedly as I hugged her tight. God, how I would miss this while she was away doing her press tour.

"That was nice," I said dreamily.

Spencer chuckled. "So, I passed the friend test?"

"Absolutely! It was lovely. All the talking and dinner stuff. Just relaxing with you and having a great evening out," I breathed.

The car ride back to the hotel was short, and soon we

were back in the safe confines of Spencer's hotel suite. As we continued chatting and reminiscing about the night, I noticed that her arm had remained firmly around me the entire time.

Throughout the day, Spencer had displayed a level of tenderness towards me that was absolutely adorable. Her behavior caught me so off guard, I barely recognized the touchy-feely Spencer as the same girl I had met the week before. She was uncharacteristically soft and gentle and warm, completely loving towards me. She treated me with a kindness that was so reassuring, that it almost made me tear up a little inside.

Perhaps it was our potential work separation during the move and her press obligations, I didn't know exactly, but I knew that her demeanor couldn't be explained by a mere coincidence. Everything she did was perfectly timed, perfectly executed, to fill my heart with the most awe-inspiring warmth and love. Just thinking about it made my stomach start doing somersaults. And not the nervous, I-just-went-over-the-top-of-a-roller-coaster kind of somer-saults. Good-type somersaults. The fun, enjoyable kind. The kind that make your whole body feel full and wonderful.

"Spencer," I said cautiously, testing the waters. "I think decided that I want to write when we get to LA. I know it's cliche, but it's what I've always loved, and spending all of this time seeing stories come to life on set has really inspired me."

Spencer squeezed me tight against her, her other hand rising up to join her first, before engulfing me in an embrace so tight, it almost suffocated me.

"That's amazing," she breathed, tears of joy almost drip-ping from her delicate emerald eyes. "You will be an excel-lent writer. It is what you're meant to do, no question. And this is such a happy moment. A really, really happy moment.

It's just... we're making plans. Lauren, together, our plans and goals match so closely, I can hardly believe how amazing this day has been. I finally found you, and you really understand me. You are more than everything I ever hoped for in another person, babe. I want to spend my days loving you and giving you everything I can. My time, my attention, my money... whatever you need, I am more than willing to provide for you. And now you want to dedicate your life to the words? The very lifeblood of me, and my acting? Oh Lauren, nothing would make me happier than the thought of you becoming a writer."

"Are you sure?" I asked, biting my lip to stop myself from crying as I examined her expression. She nodded enthusiastically as she stared back at me.

"Beyond a shadow of a doubt," she confirmed. "But no matter what happens, just know that I'll support you, one hundred percent. No matter what. In every step of your career. You'll be a published author or an award winning script writer with a #1 fan already. I can think of no better outlet for your talents."

"Thank you, babe," I smiled. "And thank you again for a fantastic night with my friends. You really won them over."

"I'm glad," she grinned back, "though I still think Julie is hesitant towards me. It's probably because of that massive crush she seems to have on you."

"What?!" I asked with a laugh. "No way. Julie and I decided to just be friends a long time ago."

Her green gaze turned playful suddenly as she shot me a wink. "Oh, come on babe - she totally has a thing for you. It's kinda hot actually, having a girlfriend that even her friends want."

Spencer wrapped her arms around my waist, pulling my hips closer to her body as she held me tightly.

"This body is all mine though, remember," she winked,

leaning in and planting a series of quick kisses down my neck and shoulders.

"Ugh, would you look at that! That perfect smile and kissable face are so hard to resist," I hummed.

"I'm such a lucky girl, and I can't wait to get you home," she murmured, leaning in further and whispering seductively in my ear. "The things I plan to do to your naked, perfect body," she murmured wickedly.

"God, Spence," I replied, moaning as she nibbled on the nape of my neck. The sensation sent shockwaves throughout my body as my blood pressure shot through the roof. "I want to spend as much time as I possibly can with you over the next month."

"I'm worried I won't be able to contain myself around you. My control is slipping, and I'm afraid I won't be able to maintain the "you're just my assistant" facade in front of the world. And I worry about the Chris situation."

"What about Chris?" I asked, his name churning the ick-feeling in my gut.

She sighed heavily.

"I'm sorry. I should have asked you. I talked to Rebecca about a deal to bring Chris on board for the sequel to the movie we are currently shooting. That means the studio wants us to keep up this little on-set romance act."

I took a deep breath and tried to steady the slight pang that was now aching in my chest. I didn't want to be jealous. Especially not jealous of an entirely fake relationship. But I certainly wasn't feeling good about the whole Chris situation.

"Don't worry, it's not real," Spencer reassured me.

"Yeah, yeah, I know."

Spencer took a deep breath and reached out for my hand. "But...it still sucks.

"Well, maybe we can give people a genuine reason for the break up when the time comes," I sighed.

"And how might we do that?" she asked with a mischievous smirk.

"An insanely hot assistant manages to bag the sexy movie star in an off-set romance of course."

"Ooh, I do love that ending! No wonder you're an aspiring writer," she winked before continuing.

"In all honesty though, Lauren, it's not going to be as simple a that if we ever want to come out. I know we've talked about it before, but I want to make sure you really understand. My public persona is as managed an act as any role I take on. A lot of people rely on me maintaining a certain image so I can land certain roles."

"Mhm?" I prompted her to continue, slightly confused at her meaning.

"I can't be out. I mean...I can be, but coming out in Hollywood would put my career at major risk. Not only would I lose a majority of my fanbase, but I'd lose a good chunk of my screen roles, too. Believe it or not, women who date other women are not the biggest draw at the box office. If I want to be an A-list action star who lands a superhero franchise I will need to remain safely in the closet. Honestly, given everything, coming out would still be likely be the right decision, but it would change everything. God, I sound like such a stuck-up spoiled brat saying all of this, huh? The truth is...Hollywood has a lot of rules."

Her hands had been waving about in a dramatic, sarcastic display, but as she finished her sentence her features shifted slightly, crumpling as her soft smile faltered. There was a long, pregnant pause.

"I want you to have your job as an actress, your career. At the end of the day, though, I want you to be happy. I'd like to think that you feel more for me than career ambitions," I said defensively.

She caught my hand as I tried to get up from the couch, and guided me into her warm embrace. Her green eyes took hold of mine again, making sure I heard every single syllable. "Yes, of course!"

She stared deeply into my eyes, slowly exhaling until I felt her whole body relax as she explained the next part.

"I want to live openly with you, and not ruin my career. It is my greatest wish," she whispered. "Being able to go out in public together. To hold your hand and not have to worry about photos being printed in magazines and websites. To go on long walks, cuddle at home, and never having to stress about anything or anyone. That would be liberating."

Spencer must have noticed the disappointment behind my smile, and her attention quickly shifted towards me as she squeezed my hand, forcing me to make eye contact once again.

"I have this dream where we would actually get to date without all of the prying eyes, and without any concern about who we let our guard down in front of. But, everyone wants to know everything. Everyone. Everyone is curious to read about the person you are seeing. The attention is intense and overwhelming, and people look at you differently," her voice trailed off, rising a bit at the end in a high-pitched, almost panicked squeak. I could see her visibly try to push it down, but the quiver in her voice wasn't going anywhere.

Looking down towards the ground, she mumbled, "I never want to see your eyes change, looking at me like that. I couldn't stand to see a speck of judgement or judgmental curiosity, as that would tear me apart completely."

Taking a deep and steadying breath, she reached for my

hand. "I'm sorry that I still have some scars from being burned previously. I've not had the most trustworthy exes."

"Yeah," I nodded. "Rebecca told me a bit about Jen."

"I loved Jen dearly, but she ruined me when she decided that telling tabloids and magazines about what went on in our bedroom was more important than our love. Actually, if it hadn't been for the studio and their willingness to sue the paper for libel, she probably would have royally messed up that movie and my career. Don't get me wrong - there was a moment I felt truly relieved at the thought of being tossed out of the closet, but her actions caused a significant amount of stress. Especially for my team. Reputation is a big deal in this business. If not for the support of all those around me, I probably would have hit rock bottom after that whole situation. Luckily, I have only found support and love."

Spencer stopped, and for a moment I thought I saw her wince as though she'd been physically struck. She raised a hand up to the corner of her mouth, pretending to brush something off her flawless cheek, while simultaneously lifting the curtain of hair that covered her forehead. Our conversation had led us to the patio, so the lighting was better. The thin wisp of hair she'd tried to tuck away fell back across her forehead, settling precisely in the same spot.

She wiped at her face again.

Was it the evening mist?

Maybe an eyelash. Or a buzzing mosquito.

It almost looked like a tear for a moment, but I'd never actually seen Spencer cry, and it took me by surprise.

I wanted to reach out, but before I could, she shook it off.

I looked at her, waiting patiently.

Instead, Spencer suddenly erupted, all but gushing. "I cannot wait to just settle in to the home with you. Our flight to LA could not get here any slower."

"I'm so excited! I can't stop dreaming of the house and LA. Can we decorate together?"

"There's nothing I'd like more," she beamed back at me, truly excited.

"Will we take some time for us. Maybe do something daring? Go out on the town?" I asked playfully, bouncing the question off of the walls with an evil grin. I knew very well that it was dangerous for her to be in public after her date with Chris, but the fantasy was fun nonetheless.

"Yes," she purred, slowly wriggling her way into my lap. "Something daring, yes. We should start right now."

"Don't tempt me, Spence," I said, attempting to be assertive, but my lusty voice betrayed me.

"I'm being as sincere as possible, Miss Daly." Spencer cooed, her soft, full lips descending upon mine, immediately eliciting a very passionate kiss.

Slowly, she began running the pads of her slender fingers over my blouse-clad stomach, stopping and playfully toying with the clasp at the front of my pants. A large grin broke out across my face as a finger slipped beneath the elastic band of my underwear.

"Don't stop," I sighed, my body trembling in anticipation as her fingers crept further and further north. Her skin felt hot against mine, her body completely engulfing me. The way she was able to coax gasps from me with the lightest touch sent waves of pleasure rocketing through my body, building in a tsunami wave ready to crash and engulf us both, and soon, no less.

"Jesus, Spencer. This feels so amazing," I breathed between labored breaths.

Taking my hand, she led me back inside and pushed me down into the covers.

My hand gravitated toward the small of her back, her hips immediately starting to gyrate as she shifted to straddle me on the king size bed. A small gasp of surprise escaped her soft, breathy lips as I pulled off her dress and teased the sensitive underside of her breasts.

She'd felt surprisingly heavy on top of me, her curvy form perfectly accented by the incredibly soft lingerie. A shimmer of gray, white and black lace caught my eye in the low light cast by the window in the early morning glow. I was impressed by her choice in lingerie and wondered briefly if the lace fabric had a silky feel. The tantalizing thought of her perfect breasts, soft and rosy, cupped in the sexy, patterned fabric, sent an electric surge of arousal through my lower abdomen and directly to the pulsing warmth between my legs.

As if reading my thoughts, Spencer raised her body in a seated position directly above me, and sensually slid her hands over each breast, grasping the bra under-sheaths with the first finger and thumb on each hand, and gently peeling the material forward. In the weak evening light, her cleavage winked playfully. She let the straps fall downward, exposing and pinning her milky white breasts with her hands, a devilish grin flashing across her face.

"Do I get a reward for being on my best behavior tonight," she teased, feigning frustration. With that, she reached behind her, unclasped the bra, and tossed the lingerie off the side of the bed. The contrast of the soft, white skin that immediately consumed me against my own dark tan lines added an element of sensual detail to this incredible situation. I pressed my lips firmly into her breasts, and let my warm breath tease a hardening nipple. I exhaled softly, taking the delicate areola into my mouth and brushing my wet tongue lightly across the increasingly sensitive surface.

"That tickles," she whispered.

Without a moment's hesitation, I felt a sudden firm pressure on my shoulders as my back hit the mattress; firmly pinned by her strong grip. Fingers tightened, her long, perfectly manicured nails faintly digging into my shoulders as she bent down and planted small, sloppy, playful kisses across my face.

Totally enthralled with her, I marveled at the weight of her firm breasts, the subtle playfulness behind her bright, dazzling eyes that sparkled when the low light of the bedroom hit just right. Through it all, my god - those lips. Thick, luscious, heavenly, a deep rose pink that was almost sinful. So soft, so delicate, so perfect, begging to be kissed. And I kissed them with the only thing I had: an unrestrained passion to consume her entirely, every molecule. When my lips finally met the moist, supple flesh of her lips, I inhaled sharply through my nose. The sweet musk of her perfume immediately filled my nostrils as her intoxicating aroma filtered in through my lungs, swirling all about within my head like a fine glass of whiskey - burning the back of my throat and exciting every nerve it crossed. At the same time, the subtle blend of her warm breath, the faint flavor of the coffee she'd enjoyed earlier, all mixed within her hot, minty inner sanctum, and swirled across the sensitive surface of my tongue in the most unbelievable of kisses.

My God, I could stay there forever.

All of the sensations and caresses of her body enveloping me, drawing me inward, pulling me nearer. It seemed to last for hours. Days, even. I kissed her wildly, tasting her hot, enticing mouth. Her mouth covered mine, sending cascades of shivers down my spine.

After we drew ourselves apart, dazed and delirious from the passionate embrace, she simply murmured, "Oh, Lauren. My love." Her voice was raw, thick, rich. Everything a woman's whisper should be. It rolled off her tongue like honey - rich, smooth, and very tantalizing. Instantly, my entire body felt engulfed in flames, the heat rising in my cheeks.

"I love it when you look up at me and lick your lips," she whispered. "God, your skin is amazing. I want to taste all of you now. I just want to kiss every inch of your entire body. And then, finally, dive between your thighs and lick up the most delicious part of you."

My entire world froze for a split second.

Then, with the sexiest smile I've ever seen, she began crawling sensuously down my half naked body, gently massaging every curve with her fingers, dragging the rougher pads of her fingertips sensuously across the much more sensitive skin of my stomach. As I felt her full, luscious lips lock onto the small, taut muscle beside my pelvic bone, I winced. The pain caused a sharp gasp to explode from my lungs as I involuntarily contorted my spine, while she held on tenaciously, the pain slowly subsiding.

Once I'd begun to calm, the numbness and pain transformed into some of the most incredible feelings I've ever experienced. Erotic rushes of warmth flooded my nether regions, my back slowly unwinding as the intense but brief sensation of her lips coaxing the succulent, delicate skin of my inner thigh.

I was hypnotized as she looked up towards me, staring directly into my soul as her lips and tongue dance their way slowly to my hidden depths, through the black strips of lace that cling so tightly to my beautiful naked flesh. She stopped just before her mouth would have touched the crease between hip and thigh.

So close that I could feel the movement of her lips forming the words, her voice hot as she said softly, "Don't you dare cum yet, Lauren. Just hold still. Close your eyes and just take this in."

As soon as the words had flown from her lips, her mouth

formed a tighter seal, devouring me completely, slipping dexterously under the lace strap of my panties and, like a heat seeking missile, finding the thin, soft fleshy sliver of skin that led directly to my aching mound.

Spencer paused, my leg folded under me; one long, slender arm crossing my pale stomach to pull me towards her. I hadn't noticed at first, my eyes closed as I reveled in the glorious feeling of the movement of her hot, wet lips against me, but Spencer's arms were bare as well. Perfectly manicured nails dug deeply into the soft skin of my hip bones, her face pressing into my thigh as her mouth fully engulfed me and her nose began to inadvertently tease the bare skin. Her wild, curly locks of brunette clung to my belly button, filling me with excitement as her hands coaxed me completely open. One long finger gently probed my lips, growing greedily with each gasp.

I reached down and tentatively stroked her dark ringlets. She rose gently, and as her eyes met mine, smiled, and quickly lowered her face to plant another series of long, sensual kisses on my thigh. Then the underside of my knee. Even the upper inside arch of my foot. With each caress, my breath quickened, though I simply let her linger, watching as she placed another kiss on my thigh, dangerously close to my opening.

A slight smirk played across her lips, her vibrant, gorgeous, sparkling green orbs staring directly into my own as her fingers worked along my body. A single finger slowly slid past my lips, deep inside with an incredible movement of her knuckles, and my insides writhed involuntarily with the combination of pure pleasure. Tingles exploded from my fingertips, all the way to the back of my skull. I shuddered, letting out a single moan and allowing my entire body to relax against the soft coverings of the massive, king-sized bed.

The deliciously wicked grin spread further across her rosy lips, her smooth, defined features seemingly dancing as the skin wrinkled teasingly. She bowed down, and her wild hair spread itself over my body, the beautiful, wavy locks spilling like silk over my bare stomach as her tongue lashed out, wet and rough, encircling my stiffening pink nipple, and then curling into a hard point and thrusting into my nipple, hard. The pain was delicious and exhilarating, as my body writhed with sensation after wonderful, pleasurable sensation, convulsing all around her finger. I cried out in a mixture of pleasure and pain, but she was relentless. Gingerly, using her tongue, she spread my legs wider, revealing the blushing pinkness of my throbbing center and the sticky, sweet secretions between my quivering legs.

Her other hand traveled upwards, smoothing the soft hair against the mattress while cupping and hefting the bottom of my supple breast, pausing only for the briefest of moments before her finger sank again into my wet mound, and her mouth encircled the aching peaks of my hard, pink nipples. The resulting flood of creamy juices that had been released from inside me flowed between her fingers, and I bucked and writhed uncontrollably under her mouth and fingers. But instead of coaxing me gently to a climax, she moved gently from my wetness, dragging a glistening, moist line from the cleft of my mound to my abdomen. Her body crawled slowly up the mattress, her long, toned limbs fully exposing her nakedness.

Perfection was not too strong a word to describe her incredible form as I marveled at the lush curves and peaks of her flawless body. A small, defined waist turned inward, and her well-proportioned, firm breasts rested proudly on her chest, while the dark, tempting red of her areolae towered well past her pink-tinged nipples.

Bold, long freckles were scattered across the creamy,

supple white of her skin, some seeming to rise a distinct purple hue. As I reached out, delicately tracing an index finger along the contours of her subtle back dimples, I felt her tense up; no doubt a slight wave of initial apprehension flooding her every sense as she awaited my next move. My hand traced upward, and pulled her entire frame into my body, fully consuming and enveloping us into an utterly tight and intense embrace. The intoxicating mixture of sensations was overwhelming.

It was as though I could feel every inch of her satiny-smooth skin against mine.

Her body was utterly, impossibly, incredible, and I could feel the sheer smoothness of her naked flesh pressed directly into the most intimate of places. Our arms clung tight about one another as our fingers intertwined, and locked behind each other's backs.

We melded together until it was impossible to tell where I ended and she began.

For a moment, there was no lust, no sexual pleasure, and every bit of anxiety or apprehension seemed nonexistent. It was just a perfect and totally unexpected moment of fulfillment as the warm embrace of the one person I felt most connected to simply engulfed me in a warm glow of comfort. In that moment, I felt as safe and content as I had ever felt in my entire life, and yet simultaneously ignited and electrified at the sheer anticipation of what was to come.

"Lauren, my love," Spencer whispered lightly, my hot breath searing into her skin. I moved my face in close to her neck and started planting soft, slow kisses, nibbling and suckling my sensitive skin.

I began tugging on her earlobe with my teeth, loving the way her whole body reacted. Her hands ran down the soft skin on my back and I moaned as her mouth kissed my neck and shoulders.

"No one's ever touched me like this before, Lauren," Spencer murmured. "Your fingers drive me absolutely wild.

"It's new to me, too," I whispered in reply. "God, I really, really love you, Spence."

"I love you, my dear," she whispered. "You are everything and more than I'd ever dreamed. You are beyond perfection."

Tension was mounting. My heart was trying to beat right out of my chest. I could feel its pounding pulse, like a frantic and terrified wild animal was trapped inside my ribs. Her hands rubbed my thighs, gently. Then up my sides, over my breasts, across my cheeks, neck, and collarbones. Our kissing became hurried. The breathing faster. Hands moving eagerly. Then suddenly there was a complete immobilization. It was like the room just froze as our eyes locked in such an intense stare. It seemed we were searching for something, then the briefest nod. Somehow it made perfect sense. We knew immediately and simultaneously that we were entering completely new territory, and there were new rules and boundaries.

Everything was charged.

Amplified.

Sensitive.

"Get up here," she moaned, grabbing at my thighs with her strong hands and pulling me onto her. "I need to taste you."

As I straddled her face, I could almost feel my heartbeat in my clit. As I was lifted in the air by her strong shoulders settling me into place, I could feel my heart rate climbing, as if trying to keep up. There was anticipation and excitement at every touch and each sense was alive and hungry for more. Her delicate touch and kiss sent me soaring, trembling in ecstasy. Her touch was instantly burned in my memory; the fullness that filled all the empty, lonely spaces, the safety she provided, the security, trust, love...

I had settled myself upon her warm and welcoming lap, clutching her to me, feeling as much as possible. Wrapping her body around mine. She ran her hands down my naked back, from neck to the crease of my hips, clinging to me in utter bliss. Tightening her embrace, she buried her face in my breasts; I cradled her head, lifting it to meet mine, tasting a tear as she kissed me. Sweet, salty. There was a trembling smile upon her lips. I kissed her closed eyes and held her head tightly to my chest. I would hold her there, forever, if that was what she needed.

After a long while she returned the gesture, raising her head. Our eyes met, and once again were lost in the eternity of the universe. It was so easy and simple to see, when a lifetime had passed, in one surreal moment.

This was real.

I'd never realized how short, and small life could be.

"Hold on to me, Spencer. Please, never let me go. I am yours, now and forever," I mumbled through the sweaty, salty mess of our bodies.

I woke up the next day in a daze, almost hoping it was a dream that would somehow slip past my hazy recollection of the previous night. As soon as she felt me stir, she pulled my naked body closer to hers, and draped my thigh over hers.

I could get used to waking up like this everyday.

This was happiness.

26

IT WAS Spencer's last week on set - and mine as well, as I'd given my notice the prior week. The final shooting days were upon us, and as expected, it was quite the production. There was a lot of singing, crying, and emotional outbursts. After 10 grueling hours on Friday, the director called "Cut!" and announced that the production was wrapped.

A loud cheer rose from the cast and crew, and everyone rushed to embrace one another. Some shed tears, as if it was the end of an era. Maybe for many of them, this was the end of something really big.

I guess it was an end of an era for me as well.

By next week, I'd be off to LA with Spencer, having said goodbye to this campus, my friends, and life here.

There were wrap parties planned for the entire week-end, but Spencer and I weren't sticking around for any more than she was obligated to attend. We had a flight to catch early Monday morning, and a moving truck was scheduled to pick up my belongings for transport to Spencer's home in Los Angeles.

Given that it was very late when the shoot wrapped, and after a long goodbye train with the makeup and hair team, I drove home. Spencer and I had decided to spend our last few nights here slow so that I could have time with my friends and she could be on call for last-minute media commitments while the cast was all still in the same city.

We'd have all the time in the world to be together once we were in LA, and I wanted to cherish these last few nights with Allie and Julie.

Two days, a lot of tears, and way too many margaritas later, I'd packed the 10% of my old life that I wanted to keep and boxed up the other 90% to give away.

A fresh start sometimes began with a half-empty suitcase.

———

AFTER FINISHING up dinner and putting the last of my belongings in bags and suitcases for our flight in the morning, I started to lock up the house for the last time. Spence and I were exhausted, and still, there was a long, tiring journey ahead.

What a crazy week.

Once it finally ended, I would be living in a beautiful home, and now, with the last box checked off the growing to-do list, I was more than ready to jump in the car and head for the studio's private airfield just out of town. The adrenaline of this weekend had already made me feel high, but the news of our flight brought an extra kick of exhilaration.

"Everything is all packed. The moving company will ship the rest of your items here and unload everything into a storage space in LA in the next few days.

"The movers can pack the small amount of things from my apartment. Honestly, most of my furniture here can be donated. There's no point in bringing my bicycle, coffee maker, or other odds and ends."

"Whatever makes your stress level the lowest, babe," Spencer insisted before glancing down at her phone, now blasting her calendar alert. "Ah, damn. I have to get going to that cast wrap party for Chris and I. Are you sure you don't want to come?"

"I'm sure," I nodded. This was a party where pictures of Spencer and Chris were being arranged to leak, and I definitely didn't need to be in a room where my girlfriend was on a fake date with her PR boyfriend.

"Okay, I'll be back a little bit later. Call me if you need anything, I promise I will pick up."

We shared a kiss at the door as I said goodbye to Spencer.

Excitement rose up within me as I realized that by this time tomorrow, we would be in LA. We would be able to forget about Spencer's work for a while, and concentrate on us, just being together.

Our real life could begin.

We could start planning.

———

Spencer and I arrived at the airport the next day, and boarded the studio's private jet. A handful of the talent and producers were flying home together, and we'd been able to hitch a ride, along with Rebecca.

On the way, Spencer filled out some paperwork, schmoozed the producers, and took a few important phone calls. When she was finished, she walked over and took a seat on the loveseat across the aisle.

"Everyone is excited that you're coming back home with me," Spencer said, her hand on my thigh as we sat on the airplane a short time later. "You're going to get to meet the whole team when we get back to my place!"

"The team?" I asked. "I thought Rebecca was your team?"

"Well, sure, I couldn't do anything without her," Spencer replied, smiling. "But I also have a team of people who take care of all the rest of the stuff I don't have time for. My publicists, my house manager, my stylist and her assistant, and just general staff."

"Wow, ok," I said, taking a deep breath. "Sounds exciting."

"There is always a lot going on, that's for sure. But, I promise, you'll love everyone, and I've trusted them all for years, so you can too."

I'd known and realized that Spencer and I led very different lives, but the reality of just how different was becoming more and more apparent. I wondered how that would pan out after we settled in.

Rebecca, who had hopped a ride with us back to her LA office, plopped down beside us in the back of the plane's lounge.

"Well, looks like the pictures from the wrap party finally hit the rag mags," she said, handing over her iPad to Spencer to flip through.

Spencer held it between us, and scrolled through headline after headline of "#TeamSpris" or "On Set Romance" reports from blatantly made up "sources." I could feel my chest tighten as we saw picture after picture of Chris with his arm draped over Spencer's shoulders in a crowd of the cast and crew.

And then, we scrolled to the main picture setting social media on fire: a snap of Chris and Spencer outside of the cast's hotel and, frame by frame, the paparizzi caught the moment Chris leaned in and planted a kiss on Spencer.

I felt my breath catch in my chest.

Of all the things I had expected and prepared myself for, this was not one of them.

This felt different.

I looked over at Spencer with wide eyes as she turned towards me.

"Well, these look pretty realistic," I started, not quite sure what to say. All sorts of emotions ran wild inside of my chest.

This was the deal, after all.

And I knew that there were going to be pictures and PR pushes.

But actually seeing them? Actually having to look at my girlfriend kissing someone else? Someone that people "shipped" her with?

This was a level of discomfort I hadn't expected.

"Babe, that is NOT what it looks like - I promise," Spencer sighed. "He didn't even actually kiss me. They're pros at grabbing the most scandalousintoeachother's looking pictures."

Her smile melted slightly. Her lips pressed tightly against each other.

She reached across the couch until only inches separated us. We sat silent for several seconds while staring intently into each other's eyes. Our fingers interlocked tight enough to almost hurt. It wasn't painful exactly – more intensely intimate.

"I know it's all just for the movie's PR, but it's still freaking weird seeing you on even a fake date with Chris," I groaned.

Spencer burst out laughing. "Trust me, he's not my type," she said, leaning over and planting a wet, sloppy kiss on my cheek. "Besides, it's not like you have anything to worry about. I've only got eyes for you."

"Right, but still," I replied, feeling my cheeks flush. "It's just so weird to see all those pictures of the two of you on some fake date. I mean, look at that one...you guys really did seem pretty close!" I pointed toward the screen displaying the photo of him kissing her goodnight.

"How much longer does it have to go on?" I asked, trying to ignore the knot now tightening in my throat. I didn't want to be this girlfriend - especially on our flight to our new home and life together, but I couldn't help the churn of anxiety and jealousy in my core.

I had been trying to avoid the gossip sites, but there was only so much I could do. Everywhere I looked, there were articles about Spencer and Chris. It seemed like the PR team had been running wild.

They had started off with small things - holding hands at a movie premiere, a photo op on the beach, a coffee date at a cafe.

But now, the media had exploded. They were talking about an on-set romance, a whirlwind romance, and the perfect Hollywood couple. Pictures showing kisses back-stage during interviews...pictures taken right behind closed doors ...the tabloids claiming its true love story..."

"We've only got a few more weeks of it, and then we're done for a very long time before the film premiers. Then, they'll make up some breakup story and we'll be free to not have to see or deal with Chris until the next movie."

"That's good news, I guess," I said, still a little unsure.

Spencer grabbed my hand and squeezed it. "It's not forever, and it's not real. Just think about what it will be like when we get to LA, and you can come and go as you please. You won't have to hide anymore."

"Yeah, that part does sound nice," I admitted.

"And, hey, maybe we can take a trip now that the film is wrapping up," she suggested, running her fingers over my forearm.

She was trying to soothe me, but for some reason it

wasn't working this time. I had a bad feeling in my gut, and I just couldn't get it to dissolve.

Something felt wrong – even though nothing else ever bothered either of these women—but today something about seeing the machine of the media marketing made me feel queasy.

Some bubble had burst.

27

It was nearly an hour drive from the small private airport where we landed to Spencer's house.

My jaw dropped as we pulled up the paved driveway. I couldn't help but marvel at the sheer size of the impressive, sprawling mansion. With white walls, huge glass windows, and carefully manicured lawn, it looked like it belonged in a Hollywood lifestyle magazine.

Spencer, naturally, had barely glanced at her enormous home, breezing past the double-height ceilings, sleek and modern furnishings, and state-of-the-art kitchen to show me up to her bedroom. Not that I had gotten a chance to appreciate the view, as Spencer tugged me in its direction. I didn't get a chance to even admire the elegant, spiral stair-case or the large pool, before I found myself pinned in the middle of the fluffy, king-sized bed, my girlfriend's lips all over me.

"We should probably make sure the van arrived with all of our stuff," I said between kisses.

Spencer gave a grunt of pretend frustration and wrapped her arms around me, pulling me closer to her. I suppose I could've at least pretended not to notice that our new location afforded her extra inches of facial features as she smiled down at me.

"You're right, you're right," she sighed with an over the top dramatic flare. "And everyone will be stopping by later to catch up. But, I wanted to get at least a good first kiss in our new home to celebrate."

I arched an eyebrow. "Just one kiss, huh?"

"Mhm," she moaned into my mouth. Grinning, she moved to planting kisses on my cheek and down my jawline. "And a third, and fourth, and fifth kiss."

Her hand lingered on the side of my hip, and I drew my body towards her. Spencer slowly sat up and grabbed my hand, coaxing me up with her, both of us reluctantly breaking the momentary spell.

"Alright, aright. But we're definitely picking this back up later," she smiled into my lips, "how about I give you the grand tour of your new home."

"So, this is the master bedroom, the ole pride and joy," she chirped happily.

It was almost surreal when my eyes finally registered my surroundings as my head tilted forward. The lush, comforting grey, a tad smoky, and the undeniable, soft creme, accented beautifully the pristine 10x7 marble squares of the floor. Crisp and modern furnishings followed, nothing terribly out of the ordinary. Other than the massive fireplace tucked deeply and off center to the far wall, unneeded in California with the absence of cool, winter months, but still, offered an incredible statement.

Beautiful, I noted.

The furnishings were fresh, and dare I say, even posh. On the long, off-white couch were two plush, and, over-the-top, unessential pillows.

"You really love pillow, don't you?" I teased, nodding towards the piles on the sofa, the chairs, and the gargantuan king-sized, cloud of a mattress and the six pillows stacked up top.

"Well, I needed something to cuddle with before you appeared in my life," she laughed. "If it's too much, or overwhelming we can change it though..."

"Are you kidding? It's gorgeous," I replied. "I love it. The color scheme, texture of fabric. Well done."

"Well, my designer, Janine, is paid rather well to oversee and revamp my place every few years," she replied. "The point, gorgeous, is the entire house is completely yours, all yours. Seriously, Sweetie. I want you to feel entirely at home here."

"You're fantastic," I whispered. "Now, how about we continue this house tour?"

The doorbell rang right as the words left my mouth.

"That should be the team!" Spencer exclaimed. "Perfect timing! We can see what everyone is feeling and order some food."

As Spencer ran off to answer the door, I sat back in the kitchen, suddenly nervous for the first time all day.

We made our way back into the open-concept main floor as Spencer answered the door. The immaculate kitchen seemed larger somehow and even starker in cleanliness in the waning natural light. If I listened closely, I could almost hear a crisp, high-pitched hum of pristine energy all around me, electric and nervous.

This was my first time really immersed entirely in Spencer's world.

"Welcome, welcome back everyone!" I heard Spencer call from the foyer. "Oh my gawd! I have missed you all!"

I heard the excited sounds of friends who had been apart for months reconnecting in the next room. The squeals of joy echoed through the minimalist hallways and brought some life to the space.

"Why don't you guys go out by the pool. It's so nice out today. Let me put on some music, and grab some refreshments for everyone."

"Can I help?" I chimed in as Spencer made her way back towards the kitchen.

Spencer nodded her head and smiled. "Please! Can you get some snacks for the poolside? There should be some chips and salsa in the pantry."

I walked over to the elegant wooden structure and pulled out a handful of freshly stocked snacks. As I was searching for bowls, I felt a sudden presence behind me. There was a soft sigh, and then warmth encircled my waist and slowly crept up my bare stomach.

"Come here," Spencer murmured, embracing me, pulling me back into the counter behind me, and resting her chin on my shoulder. Her body melded perfectly into mine, our curves fitting together like a jigsaw puzzle. I let out a contented little sigh and allowed myself to revel in the heat radiating off her chest into the back of my flimsy camisole. She was everywhere.

"I hope this isn't too overwhelming - having people over so soon. It seemed like a good idea at the time, but now I just want you all to myself. And, we have a lot of big personalities on our team."

"I'll be alright," I replied with a smile. Somehow she understood without me saying anything at all.

Slowly the arms around me retracted and her fingers danced playfully on the backs of my shoulders, twirling down the skin on my arms and eventually entwining with my own. In one swift and seamless motion, she led me out of the kitchen to a high top counter along the wall. With a comforting smile, she slipped something from her pocket and placed it in my hands.

"Well," she whispered warmly as she kissed my cheek, "I

bought a multi-part gift and completely neglected to give youPart 1 last night. Part 2 later tonight.."

I was completely awestruck.

My jaw practically hit the floor as I began to examine the object that had been placed into my cupped hands.

As my fingers lightly traced the beautiful, engraved lines of an ornate key hung on the chain of a necklace, I looked up at Spencer with wide eyes. "It's beautiful, but what does it go to?"

"Later," she whispered, running her thumb across my lips.

God. One touch from this girl and she still made me feel like my knees would give out.

I was about to pull her into the room behind us when we were interrupted.

"Spencer!? Hello? Anyone around here? Where is that movie star I adore so much?" The male voice floated around the corner. "And not to mention the beautiful and talented Lauren we have been hearing so much about?"

"Brian? Mark?" Spencer exclaimed as she rushed forward.

I watched as they embraced, as my hands smoothed my shirt. It was game time. First impressions mattered when meeting the friends.

"Lauren! I want you to meet Brian, my wonderful stylist and favorite guy on earth and his favorite guy, Mark," Spencer gushed.

"Oh, honey," he laughed. "If I'm the best of them, men are screwed."

I instantly liked the man.

His boisterous, over-the-top voice and energy melted the tension right out the window, his appearance taking the burden of the attention.

"Lauren, wow, I've heard so much. That dress fits you

perfectly." Brian fawned, his face animated. His lips glimmered a glossy, coral pink, almost matching the stylish dress pants and polo shirt combo. Slightly out of his age-range and very New England frat boy. Ironic for a Cali twink.

Brian flashed me his warm, pearly whites. My face flushed a thousand shades of hot-red, making my freckles and sunburn blush and mix. Instantly, my demeanor went from wracked nerves to a sense of calm and ease. He had a good energy about him that took the edge off.

"Don't listen to him too closely, hun. He tends to hit on everything that walks," Spencer chirped, batting a hand in Brian's direction, immediately swooping an arm around my waist as we hovered in the kitchen doorway. "Can't keep his hands to himself either."

Brian was all arms, flapping and flying all over the place as he animatedly recounted the day of the audition.

"Oh, you have met the one woman, no hold bar hussy from hell..." Brian squelched between his cherry lips, his gloss glistening, hands back in the air flying about as though he were casting a spell.

As he continued to talk at me about people I didn't even know, the doorbell rang once again. Spencer hopped up and went to collect the next guests to arrive.

As Brian continued on with his story, in walked Rebecca flanked by a striking woman who strolled in, arm-in-arm with Spencer. "Everyone, Rebecca and Tara have arrived!"

Tara. I'd never heard that name before.

She was a tall, slim, stoic woman. She had a severe hairstyle, which was pulled back in a tight ponytail. Her icy, piercing gaze and rigid posture were intimidating.

She walked and stood beside me without so much as a hello.

"So, how did you and Spencer meet?" I asked, hoping to

get to know Tara better. It was clear they were close, though I'd never hear of her before.

"Oh, I work in conjunction with Rebecca," she waved a hand in the air dismissively, "you know Rebecca."

"Right, right," I nodded still entirely unsure what her role was. For as gregarious as Brian was, she was making me work for this. "So, you're a manager as well? Or an agent?"

"I'm the house manager and Spencer's main LA-coordinator," she replied with shrug. "Basically, whatever she needs while she's in town - I handle."

"Hey, ladies! How about some drinks? I could whip some up," Brian chimed in, thankfully breaking the tension.

"Brian and I will handle the bar!" A small hand snaked into the curve of my hip, a small tug of familiarity as Spencer nudged past, smiling.

Brian shimmied, bobbing his head up and down as he clapped his hands together wildly. "Would someone do the pleasure of starting the music, please? Are we going to party?"

"Lauren, will you do the music honors, babe?" Spencer called from across the room.

"Sure," I replied before suddenly realizing I had no clue where the stereo was or how to get the sound system started.

"Here," Rebecca's familiar voice appeared in my ear. She must have let herself in during the commotion. "I'll show you how to set up the Bluetooth speakers."

She led me from the main entertaining area into a the back home office with a control panel that managed the entire house.

"You're going to have to give Spencer some slack today," Rebecca murmured my way. "She's nervous. And when she gets nervous, she overcompensates by being the life of the party."

"Nervous?" I asked. "What would she be nervous about?"

"After what happened with..." Rebecca turned to face me, now back in the kitchen. "Just humor her today, and she will be on her best behavior and back to normal tomorrow."

With one last sideways glance, Rebecca vanished into the living room, leaving me to make my way around the brightly lit kitchen. I could read Rebecca better than I could understand Spencer, but when put together, the puzzle piece fit snugly. Not in a way that anything had been concealed or misrepresented in my mind. More of a way that some matters were private, and perhaps, I wasn't ready or needed to know those components. As though Spencer's inner workings were a well-oiled machine, and I was just starting to discover them myself.

So far, I have only managed to comprehend the key functions: Spencer held on to things.

With purposeful strides back to where everyone lounged by the pool, I understood that much of what Rebecca had revealed to me about Spencer. Only recently has there been a shift in who, or what, Spencer trusted. This whole sharing a life thing was still new for her.

"Another margarita, my darling?" I heard a sing-songy voice call out, abruptly putting an end to my internal musings. A strong palm covered the taut skin of my stomach with a careful yet meaningful tenderness. Spencer shot me a broad, happy, gleaming grin as she rocked the side of her body into me.

"Sorry, yes. I need one." She nudged the salt-ridden rim of the glass toward my mouth. A tiny giggle escaped my throat at her expression of concentration. Spencer frowned and pushed a stray curl behind my ear. I didn't realize she was such as dedicated bartender. Then the cold, frozen slushy, salty, lime margarita tingled my lips. I winced in mock annoyance, wiping the remaining specs of sea salt from the sides of my mouth. With a quick but soft slide,

Spencer's thumb followed up to swipe at an invisible drop and take it into her mouth.

"Mmmh, I'll be taking care of those for you tonight." She looked extremely satisfied.

"This one came out with less tequila than intended and is one of her weaker specialties," Brian chimed in loudly across the cozy seating area by the pool, winking an eye in my direction.

"You hush up over there. Some other more responsible amongst us want to take it slow today. No getting wasted my first day home!" Spencer added quickly, "You hear me! I mean it."

A chorus of protesting boos and empty murmurs reverberated loudly throughout the house in disagreement. Mark raised his glass and silently mouthed cheers before taking a large sip.

Watching Spencer in this setting was refreshing and hot as hell. She was relaxed but in control. At ease, but excitable with her friends.

She looked happy, and, as we settled in on the patio with her friends, I felt myself relaxing too.

This really was the start of something entirely new.

28

AFTER A FEW MORE ROUNDS OF drinks, the sun had finally set and the party was dwindling.

"We should all go out!" Brian suggested with a squeal.

"I'm down to go dancing," Tara agreed.

I glanced over at Spencer and hoped she read the exhaustion behind my eyes. After a long weekend of packing and moving, dancing sounded like misery at the moment.

"Yeah, I'm beat. You guys can all go," Spencer said. "I'm staying here. And no one is driving anywhere."

"No, no, no. Not tonight." Rebecca shook her head and waved a hand. "You two can't hide out in here tonight. You're going to be all cooped up in a few days. Come out and celebrate with us."

Spencer rolled her eyes and then looked at me. "Nah, you all enjoy. I have my own hopes for a night in with my girl."

I couldn't help but blush, and the thought of us alone made my heart race.

"Come on, Spence," Rebecca begged. "We're not doing anything big. Just going to that local gay club. I think it would be good for the two of you. It's the least you can do for leaving us behind again."

Spencer let out a laugh, and it was a sound that was becoming so wonderfully familiar. Her entire body was relaxed, and her face was glowing. The light caught the gold flecks of her eyes, and the sight took my breath away.

"It's me," I sighed, wrapping an arm around Spencer and hoping to help her off the hook with her friends. "I'm exhausted. Not much of a dancer either. At least not on moving weeks."

"Fine, fine," Brian smirked. "But that excuse is a one time only 'get out of dancing' pass!"

"You just go dance for all of us," Spencer laughed, walking the group to the front door. "I'll call you tomorrow and we can arrange dinner for later this week."

"Sounds good," Rebecca replied.

"Alright, you two. Don't have too much fun without us." Brian smirked.

"You're ridiculous," Spencer laughed, giving him a hug and then a hug to Tara and Rebecca.

I followed their lead and gave a quick embrace to the three as they began their walk down the driveway.

"Goodnight, ladies. Sleep well." Brian grinned over his shoulder and flashed a wave.

"You too," I smiled, shutting the door and turning back to Spencer.

She was grinning from ear to ear, her arms open wide. "Alone, finally. It's been a long day."

"I'm exhausted." I leaned into the crook of her neck, her hair tickling the sides of my cheek.

"You don't say? It's been a bit busy," she giggled. "I'm ready to fall asleep. And you," she said, lifting my chin. "You look beat. I'll go grab the wine, and meet you upstairs. I have an idea."

"Okay." I nodded with a shy smile, feeling the heat spread across my face.

"Go get comfortable," she ordered. "And then join me out back. It's beautiful out there, and I know it will relax you. There's a new robe waiting for you."

I watched her turn and leave the kitchen, and a minute later, she returned with the bottle and glasses. "I'll be waiting," she smiled and headed up the stairs.

I could hear the low hum of music coming from outside, and I wondered what she had planned.

"Surprise!" I heard her yell out, her hands outstretched. She looked absolutely gorgeous standing in front of me.

"I thought this would be a perfect end to a hectic day."

"Are you kidding?" My jaw dropped at the sight before me.

"You didn't have to do this, Spence," I said, looking over the hot tub.

"Of course, I did. I know you're tired, and this is the perfect way to wind down." She grinned. "So, come on. Let's relax and soak in the tub. Then we can snuggle up and watch a movie. How does that sound?"

"Heavenly," I sighed, letting her slide my robe from my shoulders.

I stepped into the hot tub, the warmth immediately melting my muscles.

"Wow, this feels incredible," I moaned.

"Doesn't it?" She sat beside me. "This is why I always loved coming here."

"Mmm," I moaned. "It's the best thing ever."

"I'll get us some wine."

I felt her rise, and a moment later, heard her footsteps as she disappeared inside.

I closed my eyes and let the warm jets work their magic on my body.

"Here you go." I opened my eyes to find her handing me a glass.

"Thank you." I smiled, taking the drink.

"Do you feel better?"

"Much. This was a perfect ending to a long day."

"I'm glad. But it's not quite over," she grinned, a mischievous smile dancing across her lips.

"What do you mean?" I asked, slinking back into her arms.

"You'll see."

"So, mysterious. Why won't you tell me?"

"Because I don't want to ruin the surprise. Trust me. You'll enjoy it. At least, I hope you will."

"Alright," I replied, taking a sip of wine.

"You look gorgeous." She reached out a hand, wrapping it around my waist. "So beautiful."

"Spencer," I

"Shh."

Spencer moved closer, pressing her lips to mine.

"Lauren." Spencer breathed her name.

"What?" Lauren whispered.

"Nothing." Spencer smiled. "You're just so beautiful. And you're mine."

Lauren nodded, feeling the tears welling up in her eyes.

"Come here." Spencer pulled me close and holding me tight.

"I love you," Spencer murmured, kissing me. softly.

"I love you too," I replied with a whimper as her fingertips grazed my neck and landed on the key I was still wearing from earlier. "So, are you going to tell me what this key is for?"

"It's for this," she replied, standing to take my hand. I stood and followed her out of the hot tub.

She handed me a robe, and we both dried off before stepping back through the open patio doors. I followed her down the hall and into one of the few rooms I hadn't seen yet.

At the center of what looked like a nearly empty den sat a gorgeous, antique secretary's desk with a locked roller top. The only other piece of furniture in the room was a tall, winged back writer's chair with a wrapped present sitting on the seat.

"What's all this?"

"Open it," she replied, motioning toward the gift.

"What's in it?" I asked, picking up the small box and turning it over.

"Open it and see."

"Okay."

"Go on. I promise it won't bite."

"You're being very secretive," I commented as I untied the ribbon.

"I can't help it. I'm excited."

"I can tell," I laughed.

I began to unwrap the package and slowly unveiled a very well-worn copy of a book. "I Love Dick" by Chris Kraus. I studied it for a moment, unsure what to say.

Glancing up at Spencer, I could feel the confusion spreading over my face. "Do you have something you want to tell me?" I chuckled.

Suddenly, her eyes got wide as she realized my lack of understanding of whatever was going on. "Okay, maybe I should have explained BEFORE you opened. This was the book I brought onto set your second day. Don't let the title fool you. This book is about utter female desire and not in any way a secret message or anything. It's one of my absolute favorites. It's all about love and potential and the female artist, and I've carried it around for years as I travel from set to set. It's always just spoken to me in a really profound way."

"Wow," I smiled as I flipped through the clearly well-read pages. They were filled with notes from Spencer from seemingly dozens of different read-throughs. "I'd honestly thought we'd both forgotten about our reading list."

"Nah, it was important to you, and that made it important to me. That's why I wanted to make a little tribute to it. I had this idea that when we'd finally made it to LA, we'd start a new list, together. This could be the first one we read."

"I love it, Spence," I replied, setting the book down and walking over to give her a quick kiss. "But what is with the rest of the room? And the key?"

"Well, the key goes to this writing desk I found at this thrift store near your old place. It was so beautiful, I had it sent back here. I figured it could be the centerpiece of your new office."

"My office?"

"Yes, well, we'll need one for you when you start working on your novel. And this way, if you ever get the urge to write while I'm off filming, you can lock yourself away in here and get inspired."

"Spence, that's so sweet," I replied, my heart swelling with joy.

"You like it then?"

"I absolutely LOVE it!" I sighed, looking around at this blank slate of a room.

"This is absolutely perfect. But, are you sure? I mean, this is your home, and I've only been here a day."

"No." She shook her head. "This has never been a home, not really. I've had my fun with this place, and I'm excited to make it a true home, with you, in LA. So, what do you think? I can have my decorator here this week and you all can build it out however you like."

"I love that. That way, we can design it to feel like home to both of us."

"I can't wait," she smiled, giving me a quick kiss. "Now, whatdaya say we find some stupid shows to binge and kick off a much needed bed-cation?"

"Sounds perfect." I agreed. "How about a nice bottle of wine while we watch?"

"I'll go grab a bottle, and you start the TV," Spencer smiled.

"Deal."

A short time later, we were all curled up in bed, our bellies full of the pizza we'd ordered, and a nice buzz coursing through our veins.

"You know, we really should do this more often," Spencer mused.

"What's that?"

"Have a lazy day," she laughed. "And spend time with friends. I was missing that more than I realized."

"Well, you seem like you're in a much better mood than last week," I noted.

"I am."

"Good. I'm glad to hear that. What changed?"

"You. I woke up feeling good about everything."

"Why's that?"

"Because I have the girl of my dreams right next to me, and a brand-new life in front of me, one where we get to wake up every day, together."

"To so many more nights like this and all the more mornings waking up together," I grinned, raising my glass in a toast.

"Cheers to that, Cheers to freakin' that."

29

THE REST of the week passed by at the speed of light. We spent most of our time unpacking boxes and decorating our newly designed rooms. It was fun seeing how Spencer and I'd taste came together to make the house a home.

"Morning, babe." I yawned, walking into the kitchen.

"Good morning, sleepyhead. There's coffee and breakfast."

"You're an angel." I replied as she kissed my cheek. "Have you heard from Rebecca yet?"

"She just texted me. She's stopping by this afternoon."

"Okay." I sighed. "So, what's the plan for the day?"

"Well, Rebecca has a few options for my marketing wardrobe, and she also said that she'd bring a selection of outfits for me to choose from for some date with Chris I have to fake this weekend."

"You're really going through with it?"

"Yeah, it's only a couple of days. Then we can come back here and spend the rest of the week together, just the two of us. Sound good?"

"Yeah," I shrugged. "I guess. Not like there's much choice."

"Hey, hey, hey." She gently tilted my chin up, her voice soft. "Talk to me. What's the matter? Did something happen?"

"No, I'm fine," I sighed, forcing a weak smile.

"Lauren," she replied in a low tone. "Tell me. Are you mad? Did I do something to upset you?"

"It's nothing. And I'm not mad at you. I just don't love this whole 'you fake dating Chris' thing as you know, and I guess I didn't expect it to keep going on this long. I thought we were done for a while after the movie wrapped."

"I know. I'm sorry. It's just the studio wanted to get some promo shots and make it look like Chris and I are spending some time together post filming."

"And that's exactly what the studio wants to see. Two A-list actors, together, looking like a happy couple."

"Babe," she said softly. "I can't do anything about that."

"I know, I'm sorry. I shouldn't have snapped. I'm just a bit cranky. That's all."

"Why don't you go take a shower or a bath, and I'll meet you upstairs when I finish up making breakfast."

"That sounds great," I sighed.

"I'll be up soon. I shouldn't be long. I'll even give you a massage after."

"Oh, yes. You know how much I love those," I smiled, leaning over to kiss her.

"I do." She returned the kiss, smiling against my lips.

"Okay. I'll go get clean and try and shake off this gloom."

I made my way up to the bathroom and turned on the steam shower. My mind was still racing with thoughts of Spencer and Chris and this ridiculous fake relationship, and I just couldn't seem to shake some new level of discomfort from my bones. I couldn't shake the feeling of impending doom that came with the fact that the whole world was now convinced Spencer and Chris were a thing.

I stepped into the hot stream and tried to scrub the thoughts away, but all I could see in my mind's eye was Chris kissing Spencer in every leaked photo that now donned the cover of every major rag mag. The thought of it made my blood boil. I felt betrayed and angry, and I knew that was stupid. I mean, it's not like she was actually cheating. She was just pretending to make the world happy and keep her career afloat.

But none of that mattered, and the hurt still lingered. My mind was clouded with visions of their faces plastered together in some sort of weird, twisted, romantic collage that made my stomach turn.

As I washed the conditioner from my hair, I thought back to how it felt when the first rumors started. The first time Spencer and I kissed, it had felt like nothing else in the world mattered. It was the first time in my life that I'd truly felt loved and accepted, and I was happier than I'd ever been. And now, those feelings were being overshadowed by jealousy and anger.

"Baby," Spencer called through the door.

"Yeah?"

"Can I come in?"

"Sure."

The door opened, and I watched her step inside, a towel wrapped around her body. I quickly wiped away the tear that had just fallen down my face.

"What's wrong, Laur?"

"I'm tired."

"Tired?"

"Yeah, just tired. It's been a long couple of weeks, and it's going to be a long couple of months."

"What do you mean?"

"This move, the press stuff with Chris, everything."

"Baby," Spencer sighed, moving closer and wrapping her arms around me.

"Shh. It's okay. Everything's going to be okay."

"I know," I sniffled, begging the tears to stay firmly out of my eyes.

Too late.

Here they came.

God, I hoped she would just assume it was shower water dripping down my cheeks.

"Come here," she smiled, stepping closer and pulling me in for a hug.

"I'm okay."

"Don't lie to me."

"Fine."

I let her hold me and felt myself starting to calm down.

"Let's get you dried off and into something comfy. You'll feel better, I promise."

I nodded and allowed her to lead me out of the shower and back into the bedroom. She helped me into some clothes and then guided me back downstairs.

"Go sit. I'll be right there," she said.

"Okay." I wandered into the living room and sat down on the couch. A moment later, she joined me with a blanket and two cups of tea.

"Here," she smiled, handing me one of the cups.

"Thank you."

"Feeling any better?"

"A little," I replied, taking a sip of the warm drink. "I'm sorry. I have no idea what's come over me."

"Don't be sorry. It's my fault. I knew how hard this would be on you."

"It's not your fault. I just need to get used to all of this."

"Lauren, look at me," she instructed, her fingers cupping my chin.

"What?"

"Are you sure you want to do this? You don't have to be okay with this arrangement just because I agreed to it before I even knew you. If it's too much, we can stop."

"Spence," I sighed. "I love you. And I want to be with you. This is just something we're going to have to deal with. Like adults."

"But if it's making you this upset, we need to find a different way. We'll figure it out."

"No, Spence," I shook my head. "I can handle it. It's just a little weird, and I guess I'm not used to it yet."

"Well, I'm not either," she replied. "But there is no way in hell I'm going to make you have to suffer through this. It's getting to be too much, and I've not done a good job making sure you were okay in all of this. Damn it."

Spencer stood up and started pacing. It was the first time I'd ever seen her mad like this.

"Spencer, it's okay."

"No, it's not."

"Look, it's just going to take a little bit of time, and we'll adjust, and everything will be fine. Don't worry. I can do this."

"But what if I don't want you to have to do this? What if I don't want to drag you through this circus?"

"Spence, it's going to be fine. You've dealt with it for years, and you're still standing. I'll learn.,.or deal with it."

"You shouldn't have to, though. This is all my fault."

"No, it's not."

"Yes, it is. I did this. I agreed to the role, knowing full well that there'd be press, and the press is what's going to put a huge target on your back. And now, here we are, and you're crying, and I'm fucking furious."

"Why?"

"Because it's not fair to you. None of this is. To what, sell more tickets to some dumb action movie? No way. This has gone on too long and too far. I'm going to figure out a way out of this. I'm going to fix it."

"But the press will just follow you somewhere else."

"Then, we'll stay out of the public eye for a while. Cozy up here where no one will ever find us. I don't care. You deserve better than this."

"You've got a film to promote."

"No, no, no." Spencer shook her head. "I have an obligation, and I've already fulfilled that. My contract says I have to be involved in press and publicity, but it doesn't say anything about how. And as long as we have the photos and interviews lined up, and we make a couple of appearances, no one can say shit."

"I don't know," I sighed.

"Well, I do," Spencer replied, her eyes flashing. "I'm going to go call Rebecca and see when she'll be here. She'll have to work some of her PR magic, but I'm sure she'll know what to do. And if not, fuck it. I'll make my own headlines. I'm the main attraction in this stupid film anyway."

"I think you should wait," I urged. "Rebecca will probably tell you the same thing."

"I have an obligation to you. No one but you. And I'll be damned if some studio is going to tell me who I can and can't date. Besides, I'm done with the fake bullshit. We're doing this thing."

"But what about Chris?"

"I don't give a damn about him. We've already discussed this, and he's more than happy to be done. He's tired of the whole thing too. I'm sure he can't wait to get back to banging any and everything with legs and even the slightest interest in his abs."

As if on cue, the doorbell rang and Rebecca's voice

called in through the intercom. "Ladies! I'm here. Ready to talk wardrobe and make you fabulous!"

"Coming!" Spencer yelled out as we made our way down the stairs.

"So, how was your flight, Becs?" Spencer asked, opening the door for Rebecca.

"Wonderful. Just wonderful. Thank you. I really needed that vacation."

"How are things in LA?"

"Hot. Crazy. The usual."

"Well, hopefully you've had a few days of sanity to settle in and rest up. We've got a lot of PR planning to do." Rebecca plopped down on the couch with her usually jittery energy bouncing off the walls.

"About that," Spencer sighed. "I'm glad you're sitting down, because we have a lot to discuss. I'm ready to burn the entire marketing plan to the ground. I'm ready to come out."

30

—————

FIVE HOURS, a few breakdowns, and multiple food deliveries later, we'd finally come up with a game plan.

Spencer's declaration of outting herself hadn't gone over particularly well with Rebecca, but she'd stood firm in her decision.

"It's time," she stated simply. "I'm done discussing it. I'm done hiding. I'm done pretending I'm something that I'm not. Either find me a way to come out well, or I'll just call the paps myself."

"Alright, alright," Rebecca conceded. "No need for dramatics. You win. Let's talk logistics."

"We're coming out. We're done with the fake dating. I'm ready to take Lauren to premieres, and show her off, and live the life we're meant to live. No more hiding. And the only reason we've had to hide in the first place is because I've been under contract for the last three films."

"What are you saying, Spencer? You're going to quit acting?" Rebecca balked.

"No, no. I'm saying, no more hiding. No more hiding who I am, no more pretending to date someone I have no interest in. I'm sick and tired of not being able to kiss my girlfriend without a million cameras going off. So, what are our options?"

"Well," Rebecca replied. "Your contract says you have to be present for the publicity. However, it doesn't specify how."

"And what does that mean?"

"It means that while you have to attend the events, it doesn't require you attend them with a fake boyfriend."

"So, you're saying..."

"That it's your choice who you go with. As long as you make the appearances, it's up to you how you present yourself. I mean, it would probably be best if you at least attended the first event with Chris to maintain some level of consistency, but after that, I can't imagine the studio would have an issue if you started attending events with a different companion."

"You think so?"

"I do. In fact, the studio would probably prefer it. Think of the drama of not only a Spencer Wolf and Chris King breakup AND a coming out story all wrapped in one marketing bow? Talk about a PR dream."

"That's what I'm saying!" Spencer exclaimed exasperatedly.

"Alright, then, I'll see what I can do."

"Thank you, Becs."

"Anytime," Rebecca sighed, resuming her endless fingernail tapping as she turned her attention back to her phone. "Now, in the mean time, let's keep these plans between the three of us. I'll get working on my end, and you all need to start doing some prep work on yours. Lauren, this is going to mean you're going to be a target for the media vultures. Are you sure you're up for that?"

"Yes," I replied, trying my best to sound confident.

"If you're not, then please speak up. I'm not going to let

you two put yourselves in danger for the sake of a few headlines. You're more important than that. Besides, it's not like you can't disappear if things get too out of hand. There's nothing the press can do once you're out of sight."

"I'll be fine, Rebecca. Trust me. I know how to lay low, and I have a feeling that's all I'm going to be able to do anyway. The media isn't exactly going to want to talk to the little assistant girl. They're going to want Spencer, and that's going to leave me in the background, which is just the way I like it. And as far as the other stuff goes, I'll get used to it. I know it's all a part of the game. At least now we'll have a chance to try and control it."

"Alright, well, either of you just say the word and we'll put this whole thing on hold. But, if you're sure, then let's get the ball rolling. I've got some calls to make, and you two need to get ready for the impending shit-blitz about to come your way."

"You got it, boss," Spencer nodded. "So, how exactly will this announcement go down?"

"Well, I think we should release a personal statement. That keeps the media storm away from you personally. You all go out of town for a few days. Enjoy the newfound freedom and soak up some sun."

"Seriously?" Spencer asked. "Your plan is for us to go on vacation?"

"Why not?" Rebecca shrugged. "You won't have any control on what happens here the moment the presser goes live, so go bask in your new relationship energy while the world explodes. That way, you'll be rested when you're ready to come home and face the cameras again."

Spencer and I shared an excited smile.

"I guess we really could use a break," I shrugged. "We have been working grueling hours."

"I could absolutely use a really cold drink on a really warm beach," she agreed.

"Great. Well, I'll see you guys later. Call me if you need anything," Rebecca smiled, picking up her things.

"Will do," Spencer agreed.

"Bye, Becs," I said, giving her a hug.

"See you soon, Lauren."

With that, she hurried out the door and we collapsed on the couch in pure exhaustion.

"Well, I guess that's it, huh," Spencer sighed.

"Yup," I nodded, glancing over at her ten-foot stare. "Can you believe this is really happening?"

"Not even a little bit," she smiled. "But, I'm glad. It'll be nice to finally have some sense of normalcy."

"Normalcy? With you?" I teased, nudging my nose against her chin.

"Ha ha, funny girl. You know what I mean. A little routine. Some stability. Just the two of us and no cameras, no schedules, no people trying to tell us what to do or where to go. Just the two of us. That's it. That's all I need. You're all I need."

"You're all I need, too."

"Good." She smiled, leaning over and kissing my cheek in a soft and tender way.

"What was that for?"

"For loving me."

"That's easy. You're amazing," I murmured.

She looked over and studied me for a moment, just taking me in. Her eyes felt warm on my skin. "So are you, beautiful."

"You're ridiculous," I blushed, shaking my head.

"Maybe," she shrugged. "But you're still adorable."

"Shut up."

"Make me."

"Don't tempt me."

"Or what?"

"Or I'll do this," I grinned, reaching over and tickling her side.

"Hey! Hey! No fair," she cried, squirming away from my hands.

"Are you going to behave?"

"I might."

"I can always keep this up, you know."

"Fine," she conceded. "I'll behave. For now."

"Good."

I leaned back and took a deep breath, letting the anxiety of the last few months slowly leave my body. "I still can't believe it."

"Can't believe what?"

"Everything. Us, this, all of it."

"What do you mean?"

"It's just so surreal. I never thought I'd ever be moving in with someone, much less the most famous actress in the world."

"Oh, hush. I'm not THAT famous."

"You are to me."

"Why? Because I'm the woman you fell in love with?"

"No, because you're the woman who swept me off my feet, turned my entire life upside down, and somehow still manages to make it all seem completely normal. You've changed my entire existence. You know that, right?"

"Well, it's only fair, since you changed mine, too."

"How so?"

"Because you showed me how to love. You taught me that I'm worthy of love, and I'm not broken or unlovable or whatever else my brain told me was true."

"Oh, baby, you've never been unlovable," she cooed, taking my hands in hers.

"Maybe not, but you're the first person I've ever felt safe with. And that's not something I'll ever be able to repay."

"You don't have to," she replied, kissing the tip of my nose. "The only thing I want from you is your love."

"You've always had that. Ever since the day I met you. Well, the day after, technically."

"Technically," she chuckled. "And I love you, too, you know. So, where should we go for our 'fuck the press' vacation? I'm thinking a house on the beach with absolutely no one around."

"I've never been to Mexico," I replied, a sly smile on my face. I still couldn't believe this was all happening.

We were both silent until then—our eyes locked onto each other, and I swore I could feel happiness as an actual presence in the air between us.

"Mexico it is," she replied. "Whatdaya say we get packed and leave right now? I don't think I can wait much longer for this beautiful life with you to officially start."

She didn't need to say another word.

"Let's go, baby."

31

3 GLORIOUS DAYS LATER, I woke up to the sounds of the ocean breeze blowing in through open windows in the beach house Spencer had found for us. Well, she'd called it a beach house on our plane ride over, but we had quickly pulled into what could only be described as a private beach-front villa.

Our private beachfront villa.

At least, for the next month.

Some industry friend of hers had leant us the keys to the castle, and I was loving every moment of this private heaven with my beautiful gal.

Raising from the gigantic, plush bed, I made my way out to Spencer's newfound favorite morning spot on the sand. She was sitting there with a coffee in one hand and her phone in the other. There was a slight furrow to her brow as she read the screen intently.

"Good morning, baby," I smiled, wrapping my arms around Spencer's waist from behind. "How are you doing?"

"Nervous," she sighed, leaning back against me. "But ready."

"You're going to be great. You know that, right?"

"Maybe," she shrugged. "I just hope this doesn't backfire on me. It's not like I'm not used to the press being ruthless, but I'm not sure how much more I can take."

"You've been doing this for years, Spence. It's your job. You're good at it, and you know how to handle it. It'll be okay."

"I know. I know. And it WILL all be worth it," she sighed. "Rebecca just sent me the draft release for me to approve, though, so it just sort of got real."

"So, today's the day, huh?" I asked, wrapping my arm around her nervous shoulders. "How does the release sound? Did Becs do your coming out justice?"

"I think so." She nodded. "It's simple, but it gets the point across. It says that I'm queer, and that Chris and I broke up amicably because we were never really dating in the first place. We were just two people who met on set and became good friends. It also says that I am now dating someone, and that it is serious, and I hope the world will respect my privacy as I navigate these new waters."

"You ready to send it?"

"As ready as I'll ever be." She smiled weakly, pressing the button to send the email off to the rest of the world. "I guess now we wait."

"I think now we relax."

"Is that so?" She smiled, glancing over at me with a twinkle in her eye.

"Yup. I'm thinking we relax and enjoy some quality time on this gorgeous beach, and maybe later you can make me feel better, if you know what I mean."

"I do know what you mean," Spencer replied, a coy smile creeping over her face. "I'm always here to make you feel better. Especially if it's in that way."

"Oh, no, Ms. Wolf," I blushed. "Don't you even think

about it. You know how I get when you say stuff like that to me."

"What do you mean? I didn't say anything."

"But you were thinking it."

"Maybe I was. You'll never know," she said with a wink.

This was the Spencer I loved.

Relaxed.

At ease.

Ready for anything.

"You're ridiculous," I laughed.

"Yeah, but you love me, and I love you, too. And I can't wait for the whole world to know it."

"Well, you've got a few more days until the world knows it. Until then, what are we going to do?"

"I don't know about you, but I'm going to take my girl inside and get started on all of those things we talked about," she grinned.

"Spence, I'm serious. What's the plan?" I asked with a giggle. "This is a whole new world."

"It is. And it's ours for the taking. And, what if there is no plan? That sounds like a perfect plan to me."

"Well, we'll see about that."

"I promise you, Laur. You don't have to worry about anything. Just come with me. Let me take care of you. We'll figure the rest out as we go."

"And you're sure about this?" I asked, one last time.

"More sure than I've been about anything in a long time. It's time. I'm tired of hiding, and I want everyone to know I'm madly in love with the most amazing woman in the world." She leaned in and kissed me deeply. Softly, but passionately. "Now, whatdaya say we turn our phones off for the rest of the week and you join me in that beautiful water for a morning swim?"

"Sounds like heaven," I replied with a grin.

"Good," she said, pulling me toward her. "Because it is."

Spencer led me by the hand to the edge of the water and smiled before giving me a quick peck on the cheek and running out into the ocean, laughing all the way.

Heaven.

I could get used to it.

ABOUT THE AUTHOR

Meredith Stone is a lesbian writer seeking to give a voice to the sapphic stories she wants to read. One of her two dogs thinks her writing is funny. She is still working on the other.

ALSO BY MEREDITH STONE

Falling For The Bride